THE NEW PENROD BOOK
PENROD JASHBER

"We got a big case goin' on up here now, Bill"

GEORGE B. JASHBER

DETECTIVE OFICE

WALK IN

Jordan Grant 1929

THE NEW PENROD BOOK

PENROD JASHBER

BY
BOOTH TARKINGTON

Illustrations by
GORDON GRANT

jT174 pr

GROSSET & DUNLAP
PUBLISHERS   NEW YORK

TO DR. WILLIAM H. WILMER

In the hope that some day he may find what for
him seems rarest, an idle hour, and that perhaps
then his humor may be indulgent enough to gather
some amusement from an account of a boy's doings
in the days when the stable was empty but not yet
rebuilt into a garage, this book, compiled in great
part at the Wilmer Institute, is most gratefully and
affectionately dedicated.

CONTENTS

CONTENTS

THE NEW PENROD BOOK

PENROD JASHBER

I

THE NEW PUP

ON A Friday in April, Penrod Schofield, having returned from school at noon promptly, on account of an earnest appetite, found lunch considerably delayed and himself (after a bit of simple technique) alone in the pantry with a large, open, metal receptacle containing about two-thirds of a peck of perfect doughnuts just come into the world.

The history of catastrophe is merely the history of irresistible juxtapositions. When Penrod left the pantry he walked slowly. In the large metal receptacle were left a small number of untouched doughnuts; while upon the shelf beside it were two further doughnuts, each with a small bite experimentally removed—and one of these bites, itself, lay, little mangled, beside the parent doughnut.

Nothing having been discovered, he seated himself gently at the lunch-table, and, making no attempt to take part in the family conversation, avoided rather than sought attention. This decorum on his part was so unusual as to be the means of defeating its object, for his mother and father and his nineteen-year-old sister, Margaret, naturally began to stare at him. Nevertheless, his presence continued to be unobtrusive and his manner preoccupied. Rallied by Margaret, he offered for reply only a smile, faint, courteous and strange, followed, upon further badinage, by an almost imperceptible shake of the head, which he seemed to fear might come off if more decisively agitated.

"But, Penrod dear," his mother insisted, "you *must* eat a little something or other."

For the sake of appearances, Penrod made a terrible effort to eat a little something or other.

When they had got him to his bed, he said, with what resentful strength remained to him, that it was all the fault of his mother, and she was indeed convinced that her insistence had been a mistake. For several hours the consequences continued to be more or less demonstrative; then they verged from physical to mental, as the thoughts of Penrod and the thoughts of his insides merged into one. Their decision was unanimous—a conclusive horror of doughnuts. Throughout ghastly durations of time there was no thought possible to him but the intolerable thought of doughnuts. There was no past but doughnuts; there was no future but doughnuts. He descended into the bottomest pit of an abyss of doughnuts; he lay suffocating in a universe of doughnuts. He looked back over his dreadful life to that time, before lunch, when he had been alone with the doughnuts in the pantry, and it seemed to him that he must have been out of his mind. How could he have endured even the noxious smell of the things? It was incredible to him that any human being could ever become hardy enough to bear the mere sight of a doughnut.

Not until the next morning did Penrod Schofield quit his bed and come out into the fair ways of mankind again, and then his step was cautious; there was upon his brow the trace of an experience. For a little while after his emergence to the air he had the look of one who has discovered something alarming in the pleasant places of life, the look of one who has found a scorpion hiding under a violet. He went out into the yard through the front door, and, even with his eyes, avoided the kitchen.

"Yay, Penrod!" a shout greeted him. "Look! Looky here! Look what *I* got!"

Upon the sidewalk was Sam Williams in a state of unmistakable elation. His right hand grasped one end of a taut piece of clothes-line; the other end had been tied round the neck of a pup; but, owing to the pup's reluctance, the makeshift collar was now just behind his ears, so that his brow was furrowed, his throat elongated and his head horizontal. As a matter of fact, he was sitting down; nevertheless, Sam evidently held that the pup was being led.

"This good ole dog o' mine's not so easy to *lead*, I can tell you!"

These were Sam's words, in spite of the pup's seated attitude. On the other hand, to support the use of "lead", the pup was certainly moving along at a fair rate of speed. In regard to his state of mind, any beholder must have hesitated between two guesses: his expression denoted either resignation or profound obstinacy, and, by maintaining silence throughout what could not possibly have been other than a spiritual and bodily trial, he produced an impression of reserve altogether deceptive. There do exist reserved pups, of course; but this was not one of them.

Sam brought him into the yard. "How's *that* for high, Penrod?" he cried.

Penrod forgot doughnuts temporarily. "Where'd you get him?" he asked. "Where'd you get that fellow, Sam?"

"Yay!" shouted Master Williams. "He belongs to me."

"Where'd you *get* him? Didn't you hear me?"

"You just look him over," Sam said importantly. "Take a good ole look at him and see what you got to say. He's a full-blooded dog, all right! You just look this good ole dog over."

With warm interest, Penrod complied. He looked the good ole dog over. The pup, released from the stress of the rope, lay placidly upon the grass. He was tan-colored over most of him, though interspersed with black; and the fact that he had nearly attained his adolescence was demonstrated by the cumbersomeness of his feet and the half-knowing look of his eye. He was large; already he was much taller and heavier than Duke, Penrod's little old dog.

"How do you know he's full-blooded?" asked Penrod cautiously, before expressing any opinion.

"My goodness!" Sam exclaimed. "Can't you look at him? Don't you know a full-blooded dog when you see one?"

Penrod frowned. "Well, who told you he was?"

"John Carmichael."

"Who's John Carmichael?"

"He's the man works on my uncle's farm. John Carmichael owns the mother o' this dog here; and he said he took a fancy to me and he was goin' to give me this dog's mother and all the other pups besides this one, too, only my fam'ly wouldn't let me. John says they were all pretty full-blooded, except the runt; but this one was the best. This one is the most full-blooded of the whole kitamaboodle."

For the moment Penrod's attention was distracted from the pup. "Of the whole what?" he inquired.

"Of the whole kitamaboodle," Sam repeated carelessly.

"Oh," said Penrod, and he again considered the pup. "I bet he isn't as full-blooded as Duke. I bet he isn't anyway *near* as full-blooded as Duke."

Sam hooted. "Duke!" he cried. "Why, I bet Duke

isn't a *quarter* full-blooded! I bet Duke hasn't got
any full blood in him at all! All you'd haf to do'd be
look at Duke and this dog together; then you'd see
in a minute. I bet you, when this dog grows up, he
could whip Duke four times out o' five. I bet he could
whip Duke now, only pups won't fight. All I ast is,
you go get Duke and just *look* which is the most full-
blooded."

"All right," said Penrod. "I'll get him, and I guess
maybe you'll have sense enough to see yourself which
is. Duke's got more full blood in his hind feet than
that dog's got all over him."

He departed hotly, calling and whistling for his
own, and Duke, roused from a nap on the back
porch, loyally obeyed the summons. A moment or two
later, he made his appearance, following his master
to the front yard, where Sam and the new pup were
waiting. However, upon his first sight of this con-
juncture, Duke paused at the corner of the house,
then quietly turned to withdraw. Penrod was obliged
to take him by the collar.

"Well, *now* you're satisfied, I guess!" said Sam
Williams, when Penrod had dragged Duke to a spot
about five feet from the pup. "I expeck you can tell
which is the full-bloodedest now, can't you?"

"Yes; I guess I can!" Penrod retorted. "Look at that ole cur beside good ole Dukie, and anybody can see he isn't full-blooded a-*tall!*"

"He isn't?" Sam cried indignantly, and, as a conclusive test, he gathered in both hands a large, apparently unoccupied area of the pup's back, lifting it and displaying it proudly, much as a clerk shows goods upon a counter. "Look at that!" he shouted. "Look how loose his hide is! You never saw a looser-hided dog in your life, and you can't any more do that with Duke'n you could with a potato-bug! Just try it once; that's all I ast."

"That's nothing. Any pup can do that. When Duke was a pup——"

"Just try it once, I said. That's all I ast."

"I got a right to talk, haven't I?" Penrod demanded bitterly. "I guess this is my own father's yard, and I got a ri——"

"Just try it, once," Sam repeated, perhaps a little irritatingly. "That's all I ast."

"My goodness HEAVENS!" Penrod bellowed. "I never heard such a crazy racket as you're makin'! Haven't you got enough sense to——"

"Just try it once. That's all I——"

"Dry UP!" Penrod was furious.

Sam relapsed into indignant silence. Penrod similarly relapsed. Each felt that the other knew nothing whatever about full-blooded dogs.

"Well," Sam said finally, "what you want to keep aholt o' Duke for? *My* dog ain't goin' to hurt him."

"I guess not! You said yourself he couldn't fight."

"I did not! I said *no* pup will——"

"All right then," said Penrod. "I was only holdin' him to keep him from chewin' up that poor cur. Better let him loose so's he can get away if good ole Dukie takes after him."

"Let's let 'em both loose," Sam said, forgetting animosity. "Let's see what they'll do."

"All right," Penrod, likewise suddenly amiable, agreed. "I expeck they kind of like each other, anyways."

Released, both animals shook themselves. Then Duke approached the pup and sniffed carelessly and without much interest at the back of his neck. Duke was so bored by the information thus obtained that he yawned and once more made evident his intention to retire to the back yard. The new pup, however, after having presented up to this moment an appearance uninterruptedly lethargic, suddenly took it into his head to play the jolly rogue. At a pup's gallop, he proceeded to a point directly in Duke's line of march, and halted. Then he placed his muzzle flat upon the ground between his wide-spread paws and showed the whites of his eyes in a waggish manner. Duke also halted, confronting the joker and emitting low sounds of warning and detestation.

Then, for the sake of peace, he decided to go round the house the other way; in fact, he was in the act of turning to do so when the pup rushed upon him and frolicsomely upset him. Thereupon, Duke swore, cursing all the pups in the world and claiming blasphemously to be a dangerous person whom it were safer not again to jostle. For a moment, the pup was startled by the elderly dog's intensive oratory; then he decided that Duke was joking, too, and returned to his clowning. Again and again he charged ponderously upon, into and over Duke, whose words and actions now grew wild indeed. But he was helpless. The pup's humor expressed itself in a fever of physical badinage, and Duke no sooner rose than he was upset again. When he lay upon his back, raving and snapping, the disregardful pup's large feet would flop weightily upon the pit of his stomach or upon his very face with equal unconcern. Duke had about as much chance with him as an elderly gentleman would have with a jocular horse. Never before was a creature of settled life so badgered.

Both boys were captivated by the pup's display of gaiety, and Penrod, naturally prejudiced against the blithe animal, unwillingly felt his heart warming. It was impossible to preserve any coldness of feeling toward so engaging a creature, and, besides, no boy can long resist a pup. Penrod began to yearn toward this one. He wished that John Carmichael had worked on a farm belonging to *his* uncle.

"That *is* a pretty good dog, Sam," he said, his eyes following the pup's merry violence. "I guess you're right—he's proba'ly *part* full-blooded, maybe not as much as Duke, but a good deal, anyhow. What you goin' to name him?"

"John Carmichael."

"I wouldn't," said Penrod. "I'd name him sumpthing nice. I'd name him Frank, or Walter or sumpthing."

"No, sir," Sam said firmly. "I'm goin' to name him John Carmichael. I told John Carmichael I would."

"Well, all right," Penrod returned, a little peevishly. "Always got to have your own way!"

"Well, haven't I got a right to?" Sam inquired, with justifiable heat. "I'd like to know why I oughtn't to have my own way about my own dog!"

"I don't care," said Penrod. "You can call him John Carmichael when you speak to him; but, when I speak to him, I'm goin' to call him Walter."

"You can if you want to," Sam returned. "It won't be his name."

"Well, Walter'll be his name long as I'm talkin' to him."

"It won't, either!"

"Why won't it? Just answer me, why."

"Because," said Sam, "his name'll be John Carmichael all the time, no matter who's talkin' to him."

"That's what you think," said Penrod, and he added, in a tone of determination, "His name'll be Walter whenever I say a word to him."

Sam began to wear a baffled expression, for the controversy was unusual and confusing. "It won't," he said. "Do you s'pose Duke's name'd be Walter, if you called him Walter while you were talkin' to him, and then change back to Duke the rest o' the time when you aren't talkin' to him?"

"What?"

"I said—well, suppose Duke's name was Walter"— Sam paused, finding himself unable to recall the details of the argumentative illustration he had offered.

"What's all that stuff you were talkin' about?" Penrod insisted.

"His name's John Carmichael," Sam said curtly. "Hyuh, John!"

"Hyuh, Walter!" cried Penrod.

"Hyuh, John! Hyuh, John Carmichael!"

"Hyuh, Walter, Walter! *Come* here, good ole Walter, Walter, Walter!"

"Hyuh, John! *Good* ole Johnny!"

The pup paid no attention to either of the rival godfathers, but continued to clown it over Duke, whose mood was beginning to change. His bad temper had exhausted itself, and, little by little, the pup's antics began to stir the elderly dog's memory of his own puphood. He remembered the glad unconventionality, the long days of irresponsible romping, and he wished that he might live those days again. By imperceptible degrees, his indignation diminished; he grew milder and milder until, finally, he found himself actually collaborating in the pup's hoydenish assaults. Duke's tone of voice became whimsical; he lay upon his back and pretended to swear and snap; but the swearing and snapping were now burlesque and meant to be understood as such. Duke ended by taking a decided fancy to Walter-John Carmichael.

The moral influence of dogs upon one another is profound—a matter seldom estimated at its value. People are often mystified by a change of character in a known and tried dog; they should seek to discover with whom he has been associating himself. Sometimes the change in a dog's character is permanent; sometimes it is merely temporary. In the latter case, when the animal returns to his former habit of mind, it is usually a sign that the source of influence has vanished—the other dog has moved away. Or it may be merely that the influenced dog has concluded that his new manner does not pay. One thing, however, is certain: when a dog goes wrong late in life, it is almost invariably due to the influence and example of some other dog—usually a younger one, odd as that may seem.

Walter-John Carmichael proved his light-headedness by forgetting Duke abruptly and galloping off after a sparrow that had flown near the ground. The sparrow betook himself to the limb of a tree, while the pup continued to careen and zigzag over the grass in the lunatic belief that he was still chasing the sparrow. Duke thereupon scampered upon an imaginary track, shaped like a large figure eight, and then made a jovial rush at Walter-John, bowling him over and over. Finding that the thing could be done, Duke knocked Walter-John over as often as the latter rose to his feet. Duke had caught the infection of youth; he had been lifted out of himself by Walter-John's simple happiness, and the little old dog was in great spirits. Of course, he did not weigh the question of his conduct carefully; later events proved that he acted on the spur of emotion and paused neither to reason nor to estimate consequences. His promptings were, indeed, physical rather than mental—simply, he felt like a pup once more and in all things behaved like one.

Meanwhile, the two boys sat upon the grass and watched the friendly battle. "I'm goin' to train John to be a trick dog," Sam said.

"What you goin' to train him?"

"Oh, like dogs in the dog show," Sam replied, with careless ease. "I'm goin' to make him do all those tricks."

"Yes, you are!"

"I am, too!"

"Well, *how* are you?" asked the skeptical **Penrod**. "How you goin' to train him?"

"Lots o' ways."

"Well, what are they?"

"Why, it's the easiest thing in the world to train a pup," said Sam. "Take an ole dog like Duke, and 'course you can't train him. First thing I'm goin' to train John is to catch a ball when I throw it to him."

"You mean catch it in his mouth the same as a baseball player does with his hands?"

"Yes, sir!"

Penrod laughed scornfully.

"You wait and see!" Sam cried.

"Well, how are you goin' to? Just answer me that!"

"You'll *see* how."

"Well, why can't you answer how you're goin' to do so much? Just answer me that; that's all I——"

"Well, I'll tell you how," Sam began, speaking thoughtfully.

"Well, why'n't you *tell* me, then, instead o' talkin' so mu——"

"How can I, when you won't let me? You talk yourself all the ti——"

"You don't *know* how! That's the reason you talk so much," Penrod asserted. "You couldn't any more teach a dog to catch a ball than——"

"I could, too! I'd put sumpthing on it."

Penrod's loud laugh was again scornful. "'Put sumpthing on it!'" he mocked. "*That'd* teach a dog to catch a ball, wouldn't it? What you goin' to put on it? Tar? So it'd stick in his mouth?" And overcome by the humor of this satire, Penrod rolled in the grass, shouting derisively.

Not at all disconcerted, his friend explained: "No; I wouldn't put any ole tar on it. I'd take a ball and rub sumpthing that tastes good to him on the ball."

"What for?"

"Then I'd throw it to him, and he'd catch it just like he would a piece o' beefsteak. Haven't you ever seen a dog catch meat?"

Penrod's laughter ceased; the idea fascinated him at once. "Look here, Sam," he said. "Let's teach both our dogs to do that. Let's go round to the barn and start gettin' 'em all trained up so's we can have a dog show."

"*That's* the ticket!" cried Sam.

Within five minutes, the unfortunate Duke and Walter-John, interrupted in their gambols, were beginning to undergo a course of instruction. The two trainers agreed to avoid all harshness; the new method of teaching by attractive deceptions was to be followed throughout the course, and, for a while, they were consistently persuasive and diplomatic. Penrod brought a bit of raw meat and a solid-rubber ball from the house. The meat was rubbed on the ball, which was then presented to the two dogs for inspection and sniffing. Both took some interest in it, and Duke licked it casually.

The ball was tossed first to Duke, who moved aside and would have taken his unobtrusive departure had he not been detained. Next, Sam tossed the ball to Walter-John, who, without budging, placidly watched its approach through the air, and yet seemed surprised and troubled when it concluded its flight upon his right eye. Meat was freshly rubbed upon the ball and the experiment repeated again and again, so that after a little experience Walter-John learned to watch the ball and to move as soon as he saw it coming toward him. After half an hour, he was almost as able a dodger as Duke.

It may not be denied that by this time the trainers were irritated. Their theory was so plausible—it had sounded so simple, so inevitable—that the illogical conduct of the two dogs could not fail to get more and more upon the theorists' nerves. Naturally, then, in spite of all agreements never to resort to harshness, there were times when, instead of tossing, Penrod threw the ball to Duke, and Sam to Walter-John. In fact, to an observer who had no knowledge of dog-training, the instruction finally might have seemed to be a contest in accuracy between the two train-ers, especially as they had found it necessary to tie both Walter-John and Duke rather closely to the stable wall. Indeed, that was the view of the matter ignorantly taken by Della, Mrs. Schofield's cook.

"I niver see th' beat!" she exclaimed, coming out upon the back porch from the kitchen. "Chainin' thim two poor dogs ag'inst the wall and throwin' big rocks at 'em to see which can hit 'em the most times and——"

"Rocks!" Penrod interrupted angrily. "Who's throwin' rocks? You tell me who's throwin' any rocks!"

"I'll tell you to come to lunch," Della retorted. "And Mrs. Williams has been telephonin' a quawter'v an hour. They're waitin' lunch at the Williamses; so you let thim two poor dogs go—if they still got the strenk to walk. Are you comin' to yer lunch, Musther Penrod, or not? Come in and try to eat like a human person and not like a rhinoceros the way you did yesterday, and you know what you got fer it, too—I'm glad, praise hiven!" She returned into the house, slamming the door.

"What's she mean, Penrod?" Sam inquired, as he released Walter-John from the wall. "What did you get for what, that she says she was so glad about?"

"Nothin'," said Penrod, though his expression had become momentarily unpleasant. "Those Irish always got to be sayin' sumpthing or other."

"Yep," Sam agreed. "Let's go ahead and train our dogs some more this afternoon. You bring Duke over to our yard, Penrod, and let's get started early."

II

BAD INFLUENCE OF WALTER-JOHN

PENROD assented, and, at a little after one o'clock, the training began again in the Williams's yard. Duke and Walter-John passed two hours comparable to hours human beings pass at the dentist's, and both the trainers gradually became hoarse, though they still maintained that their method continued to be humane and persuasive. Experiments with the ball were finally postponed to another day, as both dogs

persisted in their dodging and each refused to grasp
the idea of a ball's purpose—even when it was for-
cibly placed in his mouth and held there for minutes
at a time.

Duke had long ago mastered the art of "sitting-
up", and to-day, upon command, he "sat up" till
he was ready to drop, while Walter-John was held
up in a similar position and bidden to learn from
the example of Duke, but would not even look at
him. No progress being perceptible in this, a barrel-
hoop was procured, and one trainer held the hoop,
while the other accustomed the dogs to passing
through it. Patiently, until his back ached, Penrod
again and again threw Duke and the cumbersome
Walter-John in turn through the hoop; then held
it while Sam manipulated the dogs.

"*Now* I expeck they unnerstand what we want
'em to do," said Sam, at last, straightening up with
a gasp. "Anyways, they cert'nly ought to!"

"Jump, Dukie!" Penrod urged. "Jump through
the hoop just like you been doin'! *Come* on, old Dukie
—*jump!*"

Again the patience of the instructors was strained.
Both Duke and Walter-John could be coaxed to pass
under the hoop or upon either side of it, but each

refused to pass through it of his free will. Manifestly, they had, for inexplicable reasons, conceived a prejudice against hoop-jumping, and nothing served to remove their aversion.

"I'll tell you what we can train 'em," Penrod suggested, after a long pause of discouragement. "We can train 'em to walk the tight-rope. We could do that, anyway!"

After the setbacks received in processes apparently so much simpler (especially for dogs) than tight-rope walking, Penrod's proposal naturally produced a feeling of surprise in Sam. "What on earth you talkin' about now?"

"Why, look!" said Penrod. "Listen, Sam—you listen here a minute! We can teach 'em to walk the tight-rope *easy!* It won't be anything at all, the way *I* got fixed up to do it. *Then* just look where we'll be, when our good ole dogs get so's all we got to do'll just be to say, 'Hyuh, Dukie, jump up on that clo'es-line and walk it!' And then you can say, 'Hyuh, Walter, jump up——'"

"I wouldn't, neither!" Sam interrupted. "His name's John!"

"Well, anyway," Penrod continued evasively, "you could tell him to jump up on a clo'es-line and

walk it just like Duke, and he'd do it. *Oh*, oh!"
Penrod's eyes sparkled; he gesticulated joyously—
to his mind, the gorgeous performance was already
taking place. "*Oh*, oh! That wouldn't be any good
ole show—I guess not! Why, we could charge a
dollar for anybody to come in! *Oh*, oh! Laydeez and
gentlemun, the big show is about to commence! *Get*
up on that tight-rope now, you good ole Duke!
Laydeez and gentlemun, you now see before your
very eyes the only two tight-rope-walking dogs ever
trained to——"

"Well, can't you wait a minute?" Sam cried. "I'd
like to know how we're goin' to train 'em to walk
any tight-rope when they don't show any more sense'n
they did about that hoop and catchin' a ball and——"

"*Listen*, I told you, didn't I?" said Penrod.
"Look, Sam! First, we'll train 'em to walk the
fence-rail here in your yard. We'll take one of 'em
at a time and put him on the rail. Then one of us'll
hold him from jumpin' off while the other pushes
him along from behind so's he's got to keep goin'.
Well, if he *can't* get off, and if he's *got* to keep goin'
—so, well, if we do that enough, say so often a day
for so many weeks—well, he can't *help* himself from
learning how to walk a fence-rail, can he?"

"No. But how——"

"*Listen*—didn't I tell you? Well, when he's got that much good and learned, all we do is get a board half the size of the fence-rail and do the same thing with him on *it*—and then get another one half the size of that one, and so on till we get him trained to walk on a board that's just the same size as a rope. I'd like to know *then* if he couldn't walk just as well on a rope as on a board he couldn't tell the *difference* from a rope from."

"Well, I don't care," Sam said. "I bet it'll take pretty near forever, though."

"It would if we just sit around here and never do anything."

"Oh, I'm willing to give it a *try*," Sam said.

Sam's mother, coming out into the yard, half an hour later, preserved her composure, though given cause for abandoning it. Walter-John was seated upon the fence-rail but moving steadily. Sam distrained him from leaving the rail, while Penrod's two extended hands, applying serious and constant pressure at the base of Walter-John's spine, compelled Walter-John to progress along the fence-rail. Walter-John's expression was concerned and inquiring, and

Duke, tied to a tree, near by, stood in an attitude of depression.

"Let the dogs go now, boys," Mrs. Williams called. "I've got something for you, and then Sam has to come in and get dressed to go and spend an hour or so at his grandmother's. It's after three o'clock."

"What you got for us?" Sam asked.

She displayed a plate covered with a napkin.

"*Oh*, oh!" Both boys trotted to Mrs. Williams.

"What's under that napkin?" cried the eager Sam.

"Look!" And she withdrew the napkin, while Sam shouted.

"Doughnuts!"

He dashed at them; but his mother fended him off. "Wait, Sam!" she said. "Shame on you! See how polite Penrod is! *He* doesn't grab and——"

"That's only because he's company," Sam interrupted. "Gimme those doughnuts!"

"No," she said. "There are five apiece, and you'll divide evenly. Here, Penrod; you take your five first."

"Ma'am?" said Penrod, his face flushing painfully.

"Don't be bashful " Mrs. Williams laughed, and

she extended the plate toward him. "You're Sam's guest and you must choose your five first."

Penrod was anxious to prevent his recent misfortune from becoming known, and he felt that to decline these doughnuts would arouse suspicion. Yet he was uncertain whether or not he could, with physical security, hold five doughnuts even in his hands.

"Hurry, Penrod! I know you want them."

At arm's length he took five doughnuts, two in one hand and three in the other. Then his arms fell at his sides, and he stood very straight, holding his head high and his nose to the clouds.

"There!" said Mrs. Williams, departing. "All right, Sammy! As soon as you've finished them, you must come to dress. Not more than ten minutes."

Sam caroled and capered with his doughnuts, stuffing his mouth full, so that he caroled no more, but capered still, in greater ecstasy. No pleasures of contemplation for Sam, or dwelling long and delicately upon morsels! What was sweet to his flesh he took, and consumed as he took. The five doughnuts sped to the interior almost *en masse*. Within four minutes there remained of them but impalpable tokens upon Sam's cheeks.

"Hah!" he shouted. "Those were *good!*" Then,

his eye falling upon Penrod's drooping hands, "Well, for gray-*shus* sakes!" he exclaimed. "Aren't you goin' to *eat* 'em?"

Penrod's voice was lifeless. He responded: "Well, some days I kind o' like to save mine up and eat 'em when I feel like it." He swallowed twice, coughed twice.

"I wish I'd saved mine," Sam said. "Come on, John, ole doggie!" he added, beginning to drag the pup toward the house.

"What you goin' to do with him?" Penrod asked.

"I'm goin' to lock him up in the cellar while I'm gone. That's where they said I could keep him."

"What for? Let me have him till you get back. I'll bring him over here before dinner-time."

Sam thought this request outrageous. "*No*, sir!" he cried. "Haven't you got a dog o' your own? You want to go and get mine so's he knows you better'n he would me? I guess not! John Carmichael's goin' to stay right in our cellar every minute I'm not here to be trainin' him!"

"Oh, come on, Sam!" Penrod urged, for he had become more and more fascinated by Walter-John throughout the day. "It isn't goin' to *hurt* him any, is it?"

"I won't do it."

"Oh, come on, Sam! What's the use actin' that way to a poor dog—lockin' him up in a dark ole cellar when he ought to be out in the fresh air so's he could keep strong? He likes Duke, and he ought to be allowed to stay with him. I call it mighty mean, lockin' him up in that ole ugly cellar just because *you* want to go and have a good time at your grandmother's."

"I don't care what you call it; he's goin' to be locked up," Sam said. "And I don't either want to go and have a good time at my grandmother's. I *got* to go."

Whereupon, having thus uttered his final decision in the matter, and defended his character against the charge of selfishness, Sam towed Walter-John as far as the cellar door.

"Wait a minute, Sam," Penrod urged. "If you'll let me have him till you get back, I'll give you some o' these doughnuts."

"How many?"

"I'll give you," said Penrod, "the whole kitama-boodle!"

"*Yay !*"

Blithely the doughnuts passed from Penrod's hands to Sam's, and the end of the bit of clothes-line from Sam's to Penrod's.

"Come on, Walter!" Penrod cried.

Though his utterance was already thick, Sam protested instantly. "Stop that!" he commanded. "His name's John Carmichael, and you got to call him John. You can't have him if you're goin' to call him Walter."

Penrod began to argue rather bitterly. "My goodness, gracious heavens! He's just the same as *my* dog till you get back, isn't he?"

"He is not!"

"Didn't I just pay you for him? It's just the same as buyin' him till you get back from your grandmother's, and whatever time he's my dog, he's got to be named Walter. If you don't like it, you can give me back my doughnuts!"

"Oh, goodness!" Sam groaned. "Well, you got to quit callin' him Walter after to-day, anyways. The poor dog's got to learn his name *some*time."

Penrod, wearing an unassuming air of triumph, released Duke from the tree to which he had been tied, and, leading both dogs, proceeded toward the back gate; but before he went out into the alley, Sam was amazed to see him pause at the hydrant and wash his hands exhaustively. Then Penrod opened the alley gate and passed from sight with his two charges, leaving Sam staring, open-mouthed.

Duke trotted obediently after his master; but Walter-John still misconceived the purposes of a leash and progressed for the most part in his seated or semi-seated attitude. However, Penrod reached his own yard—the front yard, away from the kitchen— without much difficulty, and paused there, regarding Walter-John with pleasure and affection.

He sat down on the grass, a dog under each arm. His imagination stepped quietly out of the present into the gold-clouded future. He saw himself in the filtered light of a great tent, addressing in a magnificent bass voice the fanning multitude.

"Laydeez and gentlemun, allow me to interodoos to your attainshon, the great tight-rope-walking dog, Walter!" And straightway, from the "dressing-room tent", Walter-John came hopping on hind legs, white ruff about his neck. Then Penrod proclaimed: "And now, laydeez and gentlemun, let me interodoos to your attainshon, Walter's little boy, Duke, the greatest tight-rope dog on EARTH!" Whereupon, Duke, similarly hopping and similarly beruffed, came forward to the side of the ringmaster in the ring, and the three bowed low, to twenty-thousand plaudits. Anxious attendants in uniform ran to their posts to support the tight-rope, and Penrod, smiling negligently——

His bubble broke. The chatter of a brazen gong and a staccato of iron-shod hoofs—sounds increasing, coming nearer—startled him from the proud daydream. A hose-cart, then a fire-engine, then a hook-and-ladder wagon careened in turn round the corner, passed furiously and roared up the street, followed by panting boys with faces alight.

Penrod leaped to his feet. The stable was too far. He dragged Duke and Walter-John up the front steps and across the verandah; he tried the front door, found it unlocked, opened it, thrust Walter-John and Duke into the hall, slammed the door and made off to the fire.

In the cool hall, Duke and Walter-John looked at each other vaguely, then discovered that they were free. A frolicsome look bloomed upon the fertile face of Walter-John. With no motive, he dashed into a large room that opened from the hall, and knocked over a tall silver vase of lilies that somebody had set upon the floor directly in his way. Then he charged upon Duke, upset him, left him kicking at the air, and scampered to and fro for the love of motion. Duke was instantly infected; his puphood of the morning returned in full flood, and he, in his turn, charged upon Walter-John.

Both dogs had been through a great deal that day; in fact, their trainers had shown them a poor time, and nothing could have been more natural than that Duke and Walter-John should wish to liven things up after their protracted experience as apprentices in baseball, sitting-up, hoop-jumping and tight-rope-walking. They made it an orgy. The house was empty of human life, upstairs and down, as far as the kitchen door, which was closed. Walter-John and Duke engaged in mimic battle all over this empty house, and wherever there was anything that could be upset, they upset it, for Walter-John was undoubtedly cumbersome.

Exhausting for a time this pleasure, Walter-John found matter of interest on a low table in the library. This consisted of a new encyclopedia, limp-leather covers, gilt tops, thin paper, seven volumes, purchased by Mr. Schofield the week before. Walter-John dragged down two volumes, one labeled "Ala-Con", the other, "Mon-Pyx". Walter-John began to eat "Ala-Con", and Duke—all culture fallen from him now in his rejuvenation—Duke began to eat "Mon-Pyx". That is, they did not eat except accidentally, for neither of them actually swallowed much of the paper; but the effect upon "Ala-Con" and "Mon-Pyx" was none the less radical.

Growing tired of this learned work, they found some semi-edible slippers in Margaret's room upstairs, also a table-cover—which frightened Walter-John on account of the noise the things made when he dragged the cover from the table. Next, he discovered, hanging in an open closet in the same room, a beady substance that proved enjoyable. In this, as in everything, the senile Duke joined him with gusto. The orgy continued.

Penrod found the fire an unusually satisfactory one. In fact, a large warehouse, almost full of hides and leather, burned all up, and dusk was falling when Penrod, smelling intensely, again reached his place of residence. As he opened the gate, he saw Duke coming round a corner of the house with a peculiar air. There was something regretful and haunted about the little old dog; he advanced hesitatingly, seeming to be without confidence, and when Penrod spoke to him, he disappeared instantly. In the darkness, his young master could not see where, or even in which direction, he went. Suddenly a chill struck upon Penrod's spine. He remembered. Where, oh, where, was Walter-John?

Penrod entered the front hall impetuously; but paused there at once—and more cold chills touched his young spine. A sound of lamentation—his mother's voice—came from the library, and evidently she was addressing Mr. Schofield.

"You never *saw* such a house! *Oh*, if I'd only followed my instinct and not let Margaret persuade me to go to that reception with her! We had Della give Duke a whipping, because he had a shred of Margaret's best party dress sticking to his nose, and he *must* have helped that horrible pup! Della threw lumps of coal at *him* when she chased him out, and I do hope she hit him. It seems utterly impossible that there were only *two* dogs in the house. Look at that encyclopedia—why anybody would think it must have taken two of them all afternoon to do just *that* much damage, let alone all the other awful things! Della says she's sure Penrod let them into the house, and this time I certainly don't intend to say one word against it if you think you ought to——"

"Yes, of course I ought to," Mr. Schofield said; and, to the dismayed ears listening in the hallway, his voice was the executioner's. More and worse was to follow, however, because what Mr. Schofield now added was mysterious. "We'll put that thing on him, too," he said.

That was all; and there was silence except for the rustle of a newspaper, while Penrod continued to remain in abeyance, so to speak, holding his breath. He could face, albeit with an anguish of reluctance, the known punishment implied by "Yes, of course I ought to"; but what had his father meant by saying, "We'll put that thing on him, too"? What thing? How was it to be affixed to him, and where? His imagination recoiled from this unknown horror and he determined to postpone the affixing as long as he could. With infinite precaution, he returned to the front door, let himself out, and no one could have heard a footfall as he crossed the verandah.

He found Sam closing the door of the Williams's cellar upon Walter-John. "Where'd you come across him?" Penrod asked, in a preoccupied tone. He was not much interested.

"*Nice* way to bring him home like you promised, wasn't it?" Sam returned indignantly. "I found him out in the alley, 'way up by the corner, and he acted like he was scared to death. He didn't even ack like he knew me."

"See here a minute, Sam," Penrod said, in a friendly though still preoccupied tone. "On account of all those doughnuts I gave you, and everything, I don't s'pose your mother would mind if I stayed over here for dinner much, would she?"

III

PROPHYLAXIS

HE MADE a poor meal of it, for his imagination was haunted, and he had eaten but little when an imperious telephoning commanded his instant presence in his own home. Thither, with dragging feet, he returned, woefully expectant, and was not much relieved to be sent at once to bed, apparently in lieu of stronger punishment; so, in the dark he lay, full of foreboding. What thing did they design to put upon him? How would it be applied and what appearance would it give him? There seemed to be little doubt that it would be in the nature of an affliction. Then, after a long time of wondering, he fell into a doze; but was startled to wakefulness by his father's speaking in a low voice to Mrs. Schofield in the upper hallway: "Let it go until Monday morning. Put it on just before he goes to school Monday morning."

Thus, he had all day Sunday to spend in intermittent spells of dread and wonderment, for he did not dare to make inquiries; but on Monday morning he learned the truth. It had been his simple plan to leave the breakfast table unexpectedly, to dash across the room and leap from the window, as if impelled by some vagrant impulse of light-hearted merriment, and so speed shouting schoolward. It was not to be; his uneasiness was so great that he delayed his flight until his father and Margaret had gone from the house and he was left alone in the dining-room with his mother. Della had just brought her the thing that was to be put upon him, and he looked at it; but for one moment more still remained uncertain of its character and use.

Mr. Schofield was an old-fashioned man, somewhat obsolete in his hygiene, and, remembering the misfortunes of his own youth, he had directed Mrs. Schofield to fasten a stout cord about the neck of their son—to fasten it securely under the collar, and to hang a bag of asafetida upon the cord, placing the bag next to Penrod's person and concealing it from sight beneath his upper garments. There had been an outbreak of epidemic diseases among the school-children of a town not more than forty miles away, and Mr. Schofield believed in the simple, old-time precautions, even when their use required (as in this case) both muscular exertion and oratory to enforce. Penrod whiffed the powerful odor of the bag, as his mother advanced timidly with it, and suddenly he realized what was intended to be put upon him; he perceived that he was meant not only to smell this smell, thus briefly, once, but to carry it about with him upon his breast-bone for an indefinite number of days—perhaps even weeks—smelling it uninterrupt-edly with his own nose and making it his most salient, memorable and discussed characteristic in the nose of the world.

His expressions of repugnance were so virulent, and his horrified resistance was so outrageous, that Mrs. Schofield did not persist in attempting what was beyond her power, and Penrod went to school in an injured state of mind, but not wearing the bag. On Tuesday morning, however, Mr. Schofield was an hour late at his office, and Penrod wore the bag.

Finally, Mr. Schofield's capacities as a parent, a rhetorician and a strong-arm man may be calculated from the fact that his son did not dare to remove the accursed thing, but, once conquered, accepted it hopelessly as part of himself. He had been made to understand that its presence upon him was all that stood between him and dissolution; but, what weighed more with him, he believed that whether he died or not as a result of its removal, he would first have to face a reckoning with his father, which the latter had powerfully sketched in strong, terse words. So the unfortunate set forth tardily to school, not with hanging head, indeed, for that made his sufferings keener; rather, he held his head unnaturally high, moving it from side to side, like one seeking the upper airs of heaven, and hating himself and all this lower earth of ours.

Now, there is something to be said for the asafetida bag: the wearer is almost as horrible to others as to himself, and Penrod, equipped with this protection, smelled so that neither germ-bearing persons nor anybody else would willingly come near him, which of course helped to prevent all manner of infection. But a robust state of health is not the only necessity of a contented mind. Penrod was sensitive, and during the following days a continuous progression of episodes, testifying to a new-found unpopularity, increased the depression induced by his own nasal martyrdom.

His friends avoided him openly, stating their reasons. A man in a street-car sat down by him and then abruptly changed his seat, a conspicuous process duplicated by the next occupant of the space vacated, after which there was so much staring by the other passengers that Penrod uneasily left the car, preferring to walk to the moving-picture theater whither he was bound, and where he took his seat as unobtrusively as possible, but not without dislodging a party of ladies. "Let's get out to the *air !*" said their leader. And the little octoroon girl whose desk was in front of Penrod's at school publicly requested, and obtained, a change of location on the ground of faintness.

Even at home, his own father, tyrant but diplomatist as well, contrived to be very little in the same room with him; while Margaret was most offensive of all, reaching near to tears merely because he came and sat with her when some young men were calling. And one calm, bright morning, on his way to school, he encountered two sweet-faced women upon the sidewalk, and heard one of them say, "What a brooding face that child has!" and then, as he passed them, they both said, "Oh, goodness!" one after the other, and hurried on.

Then, one Saturday afternoon, as he strolled, more broodingly than ever, and accompanied by Duke, the one creature on earth that had not at least partially deserted him, he heard a lovely voice calling his name, and, glancing over his shoulder, he beheld the most beautiful little girl in all the world. She was running to overtake him and join him.

"Penrod Schofield! Wait!" she called. "I want you to come on over to our house. Wait, Penrod!"

But he dared not wait. She was, of all people of the earth, the very last he wished to admit within the boundaries of his aroma. Infamously he fled up an alley, and it was a bitter scooting, with not another backward look. He disappeared from the sight of Marjorie Jones.

She stood upon the alley corner, staring, heart-stricken. "All right for you, Penrod Schofield!" she cried to the air, which was not altogether vacant but still bore a slight, unpleasant impregnation not connected in the mind of Marjorie with the haste of her friend. "I'll never speak to you again!" she added, purely as a matter of formula, and went her indignant way.

This may have been the foundation of her theory, developed later in life, that men are not to be depended upon; but just at present she bent her conscious mind upon plans for having it out with Penrod. And having returned to her own home, to find her mother upon the point of departure to call upon Penrod's mother for a charity-committee consultation, Marjorie easily obtained permission to accompany her. Mrs. Jones was glad to be indulgent, for Marjorie had been "good" about a certain matter that very morning.

The fugitive, meanwhile, having turned into an intersecting alley, paused to watch two carpenters who were engaged in planing boards to a miraculous smoothness for a stable in process of erection near by. Nothing is much more fascinating to a boy, and Penrod almost forgot his troubles as he gazed at the thin shavings curling forth from the skilful planes that moved so steadily and with such a pleasant, crisp sound along the planks. It seemed marvelous and yet easy; he wished the carpenters would let him try; he believed he could do it. Enchained, he moved closer.

A look of annoyance appeared upon the face of the carpenter nearer to Penrod. The man became nervous; he looked about him complainingly. He fidgeted, and would pause in his work and then resume it fiercely. But Penrod, watching only the plane, and not noting the symptoms of the workman, drew closer.

"Hey!" cried the carpenter. "Go somewheres else!"

Penrod withdrew with a plaintive air. He went round the bench to where the other carpenter was working.

"No, fer goshsake," said this other bitterly, making repellent gestures, "don't come around here!"

"Hey!" said the first. "Ain't they nowheres else you can go? Go on plumb away, can't you?"

Penrod, turning his back upon them, moved dumbly down the alley, while Duke roused himself from a short nap in the pleasant shavings, and faithfully trotted after his outcast master. As if nothing had happened the sun shone placidly down upon this piteous withdrawal.

A few minutes later, the harried boy was in the act of entering the back gate at his own domicile, when an elderly passer-by of interesting appearance hailed him genially. This person was gray-haired and shabby; he had an unusually shiny, though spotted, face, and expanses of him and of his apparel seemed to be made simply of antique grease, caked with dirt. He was, in brief, the most unfastidious man Penrod had ever seen.

"Say, little boy," he began, approaching slowly, "don't you want to help an ole sojer in hard luck?"

Penrod was in a humble mood. "What you want?" he said.

The ole sojer came nearer. He had the pathetic look, common to his kind, of having been mistreated for something he had meant only in joke. His eyes became more watery. "I had a little boy wunst, almost jest like you," he said tenderly, "before I went to the war. He'd be'n jest yore age if he'd lived. Hain't yore paw got a suit o' clo'es maybe he wouldn't miss or nothin', if you could kind of go and fetch 'em out to me?"

Penrod was touched. "Well, I don't know," he said. "I don't think he's home, now."

"That wouldn't matter," said the ole sojer. "He'd be glad to have you git 'em fer me, if he was here. Fact is, I seen him down town, and he said I could have 'em. He says: 'You go up to my house, and if my little boy's home, you tell him I says to git you a coat and pants ɔ' mine. He's a good boy,' he says, 'and he'll do jest like I tell you. He'll go right in the house and fetch 'em out to you.'" The ole sojer set a benevolent hand on Penrod's head and leaned toward him affectionately, continuing: "Yessir, that's what yore paw tole me, and I can tell a good boy by the looks of him. Soon as I laid eyes on you, I seen you was a good———" Abruptly he paused, a puzzled and distressed expression coming to the surface of the shiny countenance. He sniffed the burdened air, and his distress became more poignant. "What's wrong with you, son?" he said, stepping back some paces. "What's wrong with you?"

It was the last straw. Fifteen seconds later, the ole sojer was retreating profanely from that neighborhood, though missiles continued to be hurled from the other side of the Schofields' alley-fence long after he was out of range.

Having thus assisted in demonstrating that, contrary to tradition, pariahs do not always establish a warm fellowship with one another, Penrod retired to the interior of the stable, seated himself upon the floor with his back to the wall—a true symbol of his condition—and gave himself up to revolutionary broodings. Baleful they were and dark, for this was the gloomiest hour in all that gloomy period.

They took the consoling form of visions of revenge. He saw himself at the head of a band of moving-picture cowboys, charging upon mankind in general, laying waste, burning, blowing up, leaving a trail of wrack and lamentation. He led his fire-eaters straight upon regiment after regiment of carpenters and tramps—riding down thousands of shrieking carpenters and tramps. He drew up his victorious men in front of the school-building, and summoned the trembling teachers to lead out a little octoroon girl. "There, Bill, that's the one," he said sternly to the most bloodthirsty of all his followers; and Bill, with a brutal laugh, tied a sack of asafetida weighing many pounds about the neck of the little octoroon girl. Bill's duty was assigned to him; he was to remain with the little octoroon girl for the rest of her life to see that never—day or night—was the sack of asafetida to be removed from her person.

Then Penrod rode on, a brass band marching just behind him, playing beautifully; and presently scouts reported a large body of carpenters, entrenched but quivering with fear, just round the corner. With a fierce shout he charged: "Bing, bing! Bing, bing——"

IV

MUNCHAUSEN

MUSTHER PENROD!" This was a hail from the house. Della, the cook, stood in the kitchen doorway, calling, "Musther Penrod!"

Sluggishly, a morose Penrod made himself partly visible in the shadows of the carriage-house. "What you want?"

"C'm in the house. Yer mamma wants you."

"What for?"

"C'm on in, now, I tell you!" Della cried severely.

"Well, ain't I comin'?" he returned, emerging slowly. "Needn't make all that fuss about it, I guess!" He came—but in profound gloom; and he consumed several minutes in the passage to the house, pausing to disperse a pile of fallen leaves that had been raked from the lawn. (They represented enemies, such as carpenters, tramps, little octoroon girls and the like.) Arriving at last, and by such slow stages, in the kitchen, he fixed a resentful eye upon Della, for unmistakably there was something leering and superior in her expression. He took it as an allusion to his unfortunate odor.

"You shut up!" he burst forth, though she had said nothing.

"G'wan in the livin'-room," said Della, giggling openly. "She's waitin'."

This "she" Penrod failed to identify properly, until Della made it clear for him at their next encounter, later in the day. But now, naturally accepting it as a reference to his mother, he betook himself to the apartment indicated, and, entering abruptly, demanded, "Well, what you want?" before he perceived the presence of visitors. Then he stopped dead in his tracks, stricken. Sacred and awful, there

beside his own mother, sat Mrs. Jones, the mother of
Marjorie. And there, demure and silent in a stiff
chair, sat Marjorie, herself, her hands folded in her
lap. Penrod stood and suffered, while all round his
fiery head rose the odor of asafetida. He seemed to
drown in it.

"Here's Marjorie, Penrod," Mrs. Schofield said
pleasantly. "Don't you want to take her in the
library and look at pictures while her mamma and I
have a little talk?"

Miserably he found utterance. "Well, come on,"
he said, swallowing; whereupon Marjorie rose with
an obedient air and followed him into the library.

"I'm afraid you won't mind her being in another
room," said Mrs. Jones, when her daughter and Penrod were out of hearing. "I didn't want to apologize
before her; but her father is rather old-fashioned, and
he has insisted upon her wearing a bag of asafetida—
and I'm afraid you found it rather overpowering."

"Not at all," Mrs. Schofield returned. "Penrod
has been wearing one all week, and we're getting
used to it. I hope you didn't have as much trouble
persuading Marjorie to consent to it as we did with
Penrod."

"Oh, no!" said Mrs. Jones. "I'd been afraid she

might be a little upset at the idea, but she was almost angelic about it. I suppose, perhaps, girls are different about such things from boys."

"They must be," said Mrs. Schofield.

In the library, Penrod was keeping as far from Marjorie as possible. "Well, what kind o' pictures you want to look at?" he said, moving to the bookshelves.

"Any kind; I don't care," she answered, following.

He immediately withdrew to the other end of the room. "Well, suit yourself," he said stiffly. "There's the books."

She stooped and began to tug at a heavy volume. "Here's the Bible," she announced. "Let's look at Bible pictures."

"Well, you can," said Penrod. "I don't want to, particu'erly."

"Well, come and help me get it out, anyway. Please, Penrod!"

And then, as she seemed about to approach him to emphasize the request, he became desperate. He threw one hunted glance over his shoulder. Flight lay only through the living-room. There was nothing for it but to let her discover the truth about him, that thing which he marveled she had not already perceived and mentioned; for it seemed to him that he was growing more and more redolent.

He went doggedly to the shelves and pulled out the big family Bible for her. "There!" he said, awaiting the blow; but none came.

"Now let's sit down here on the sofa," said Marjorie, in a cozy voice. "Let's look at the pictures in the old part."

Amazement filled him, and he obeyed. They sat, side by side, with the open Bible half on his lap and half on hers, and she appeared to have no complaint of him. On the contrary, she seemed unconscious of everything except the pictures, exclaiming: "Oh, look, Penrod!" or, "Here's a nice one!" or "I *do* like Moses, don't you, Penrod?" as unconcernedly as if the air were pure about them. And yet it was evident to him that he reeked as never before.

But Marjorie prattled on, and her sweetness began to touch Penrod vaguely but deeply until he remembered hearing his father say that people with bad colds were unable to smell anything. Marjorie showed no signs of having a cold; but perhaps there were colds that didn't show.

After a time she leaned back, ceasing to look at

the pictures, and her expression became discontented.
"Penrod Schofield," she said, in an altered tone,
"I saw you before, to-day."

"When?"

"Yes, you better say, 'When'," Marjorie returned
sharply. "You know you ran down that alley!"

"Oh—then!" he said feebly.

"You heard me call you! You did!"

"Well, I'm not *sure* if I did."

"You are, too! You looked around."

"Well," he began, groping for a defense, "I *had*
to. I had to go down there."

"Well, what for?"

His eyes looked dull and vague as he continued
to grope; then they brightened. "There was some
carpenters down there."

"Well, what if they were?"

"Well, I guess I was after them, wasn't I? One of
'em had called me names, and I was after him," he
improvised, growing brisker as his imagination began
to work itself into good running-order. "I looked up
the alley just that minute, and I saw he was there,
and I had to go after him, because I hadn't seen him
anywheres since he called me those names."

Marjorie was more than mollified; she was dumfounded. "Penrod Schofield! You mean he was a great big *man?*"

"Well, I don't care anything about that," said Penrod. "He was a carpenter, anyway, wasn't he? I always fight carpenters."

"Penrod!"

"I guess I'm not afraid of any ole *carpenter!* Why, lots o' boys can whip *carpenters!* That is," he added, reconsidering, "there's some boys that wouldn't be afraid of one carpenter at a time; but when it comes to me, I go after 'em, I don't care how many they are." The words came spontaneously from his mouth, and they sounded admirable.

"Penrod Schofield!" Marjorie's eyes were wide and worshipful. Neither did she question these great announcements. She knew that boys led lives strange to her, shrouded from her, and she was amazed but not incredulous.

Incited by the lovely effect upon her, Penrod continued his insanity in large and confident tones. "They better look out for *me*," he said, "when I'm after 'em! They don't come around *this* neighborhood much, I expect you'd notice if you lived next door or somewheres!"

She leaned toward him, her mouth open in fascinated wonder. "Penrod, what do you do to carpenters?"

"*Oh*, oh!" He sniffed vaingloriously. "I'll show 'em soon enough if they come around *me* much! I guess they'd find out what I'd do to 'em—soon enough!"

"Penrod, tell *me*," she pleaded breathlessly. "What do you do to the carpenters when they do come around you? *Please* tell me, Penrod."

"Well——" He paused; then his inspiration was renewed. "I wait till they try to kick, and then throw 'em down."

"How?" she gasped.

"Well, that's the way *I* do," he said, as if other boys used other (but inferior) methods of destroying carpenters. "I always ketch their feet. Ole carpenter gets his foot up in the air—look out! I just twist it around till he can't stand up any more. Ole carpenter's had about enough for one day, I guess! *Oh*, no!"

"Penrod Schofield!" Marjorie cried, for now she was all aglow with excitement and admiration. "Could you do it to anyone else besides carpenters?"

He looked preoccupied, concentrating his mind on this new thought. "What?"

"Could you do it to anybody but carpenters?"

"Well, I don't know," he said slowly. "Tramps, I could. I could do it to tramps." All at once he became fluent and brisk again. "Why, just before I came in the house there was on ole tramp in our alley, and I— well, I expect he was pretty sorry he ever came in *this* neighborhood! I caught him lookin' at me, and I says, 'Who are you lookin' at?'" (Penrod quoted himself as having used a tone of intolerable truculence.) "I went up and I ast him who he was lookin' at. 'Who are you lookin' at?' I says. 'Who are you looking at, you ole tramp, you!' I went up and I ast him, 'Who are you *lookin'* at?'"

Marjorie was a perfect audience; she was almost atremble. "Who'd he say he was lookin' at?" she cried.

"Who'd he say?" Penrod returned scornfully, "Who'd he say he was lookin' at? I guess he didn't *say* much!"

"Why didn't he? Didn't he say *anything?*"

"Well, I guess he didn't!"

"Did you twist his feet, Penrod?" she asked, in the tone of a worshipful slave.

Penrod fixed his eyes somewhat dreamily upon distance, and smiled mysteriously. "Better ast *him,*" he said. "You just better ast *him*. I don't expect you'll see him around *here* much, after to-day!"

"Did you throw him down, Penrod?"

"You better ast *him*, I guess!"

"Penrod! How'd the ole tramp look when he was on the ground?"

"You better ast *him* how he looked, I tell you!"

"He looked sorry, I expect. Wasn't he sorry then, Penrod? Didn't he say he was sorry then, Penrod?"

"Did he? *Oh*, no!" Penrod satirically expressed the extremity of the tramp's remorse. "Oh, no; *he* didn't say he was sorry! Oh, no; *he* didn't! *Oh*, no!"

This seemed to conclude the account of that adventure, for Penrod leaned back, sneering slightly at the fallen enemy in retrospect, and was silent.

Marjorie looked at him timidly, and then, in a humble tone, she asked: "Penrod, when you ran up the alley to-day after that carpenter, was there more than one?"

"More than one?" he repeated vaguely.

"Was there any more carpenters with him?"

"*Was* there!" he returned, implying carpenters in such numbers that the picture he created in Marjorie's mind was of an alley choked with carpen-

ters who jostled one another in flight. "*Was* there?
Oh, no!"

"They ran when they saw you coming, didn't
they, Penrod?"

"Ran? *Oh*, no; *they* didn't run! *Oh*, no!"

"They ran because they knew how you'd twist
their feet, didn't they? That's why they ran, I guess,
wasn't it, Penrod?"

"Better ast them!"

"Penrod," she begged, clasping her hands eagerly,
"tell me some more how you do to carpenters!"

Penrod complied. He related victorious adventures
among carpenters, allowing it to appear that he
always fought members of that vile sect upon sight.
He caused Marjorie to shudder and glow after many
a "Better ast *him* how he looked!" or "I guess if
you'd been there you'd *heard* what he said!" in response to her search for these details. It must be admitted that Penrod painted with the broadest of
brushes, producing some mistiness of effect, but (for
this listener, at least) a perfect illusion of reality and
never a doubt in the world, even when the carpen-
terial exploits grew monstrous. For, as Penrod became more and more fluent, they did attain mon-

strosity. Nothing could have been more natural. The loftiest boast follows the profoundest humiliation, and Penrod had lived through an awful week, culminating in the injurious conduct of the two carpenters who had been unable to bear his remaining in their vicinity. In the amount of mortification endured this had been the climax.

The recital for the sweet auditor at his side soothed him at first and then elated him. He strewed the field of Marjorie's imagination with fallen and writhing carpenters—everywhere she saw carpenters whose feet had been twisted, carpenters grinding their faces in the dust, carpenters howling their remorse. Within her there was a slight consciousness of something not precisely lifelike and customary about all this—but skepticism lay dormant and the flame of her trust was undimmed.

And so Penrod talked on, making up to himself for his martyrdom, and casting such a spell upon himself and upon Marjorie that though the air about them was fairly choked with the fumes they shed, they both actually forgot, for that enchanted interval, that there was such a thing as asafetida in the world. Thus with Desdemonas ever; they do not need to sit in Venice when they listen, and young

Othellos long since learned that to tell of their adventures it is not absolutely necessary to have had
them.

Penrod accomplished a wholesome thing for himself by his Munchausenings—he had been in a low
state of mind ever since the bag was placed upon his
breast-bone; he had felt himself outside the social
pale, justly despised and spurned of men; but now
he restored himself to his normal condition of being.
That is, he began once more to consider himself of
the very highest importance. The past vanished from
him like a dream. He spake mightily of mighty deeds,
and they seemed to become real even as his lips
created them.

He rose from the sofa to gesticulate; he illustrated
his theme with sweeping and allegedly dexterous
motions; he enacted the rôles of carpenters, and he
impersonated himself—a threatening, contemptuous,
triumphant Penrod, hurling and overthrowing these
cravens. Then he would start afresh. "Well, 'nother
time, I was walkin' 'long, ole carpenter came up
to me——"

Marjorie passed from one suspense to another,
though the hero came forth victorious from every
encounter. She sat leaning toward him, her lovely

eyes glistening, and she began to understand, for the
first time, what a wonderful being Penrod Schofield
was. Nay, once this feeling found place within her, it
expended with miraculous swiftness; she beamed and
shone with pride in him. And at last, when her
mother was heard calling her from the hall, "Come,
dear; we must be going", Marjorie sprang up and
stepped close to the glamorous boy.

"Penrod, will you promise me something?" she
said eagerly.

"What?"

"Promise me not to go out after any more carpenters again to-day."

He frowned, seeming loth to consent. "Well, I
don't know——"

"Promise me!" she urged impulsively. "I'll tell
you a secret if you will."

"What secret?"

"No; you promise me, first."

"Well, it's gettin' kind o' late, anyway. I guess I
promise. What secret?"

Marjorie leaned closer and whispered hurriedly,
"Georgie Bassett told me you had to wear an as-
afid'ty bag——"

Penrod underwent a horrible sensation. The gossamer bottom dropped out of the glittering world his eloquence had created, and his spirits fell measureless fathoms through the hole. In an instant, the dreadful truth became actual and smellable again; he was in the abyss. And if ever he "caught" Georgie Bassett——

But it was his happy lot to ascend as rapidly as he he had gone down, and to even greater heights.

"*Wait*, Penrod," Marjorie urged, as he wrenched shamefacedly and defiantly away from her. "*That's* not it!"

"Well, what is it?" he muttered.

And then she told him. She whispered quickly: "I got one, too. I didn't mind, because *you* had one!" And with that, she was gone, leaving him alone in the room with the echo of a shy laugh, half-whisper, in his incarnadined ear.

He stood struck dumb; and the asafetida bag began to grow warm and pleasant upon his breast-bone. Something ineffable passed over him, and the smell that had been so dreadful slowly became magically sweeter. It might have been the smell of violets.

Toward dusk that evening, Penrod was out in the side yard trying to teach Duke to turn somersaults—

an accomplishment that Duke persisted in considering of no benefit to a dog—when a neat-looking man
in overalls glanced over the fence, in passing, and
recognized Penrod. It was a carpenter, but evidently he had a conscience.

"Hey," he said, "you come around and watch us
some day when you don't haf to wear that asafidity
any more!"

The spell of Marjorie's last whisper was still upon
Penrod; and he cared not how long deferred that day
of which the carpenter spake. Nevertheless, the
recollection of the curling shavings gave some pleasure and stirred him to gratitude.

"Thank you, sir," Penrod said to the carpenter.

V

BEGINNINGS OF JASHBER

PENROD did not realize that he had said anything remarkable to the carpenter; and perhaps, indeed, he hadn't. People older than he live in a world commingled of imaginings and the appearances we call realities, and live there little disturbed by constant inconsistencies. It is, in fact, a human process far from uncommon for us in fancy to insult, humiliate, or even destroy, injurious superiors, and then, perhaps almost immediately, to greet them in the flesh with courtesy, or even with a deference perfectly genuine. It might be clearer possibly to say that many of us, like Penrod, live not so much in one commingled world as in two interchangeable worlds, the one able instantly to replace the other with such smooth rapidity as to produce not the slightest jar. In youth especially, the interchanging of these two worlds is so continuous, so facile, and accomplished with so quick and sleek a movement that it is like the play of light and shadow when young grasses flutter and twinkle, reflected in a clear stream, itself unruffled by the April breeze. Penrod's interchangeability in respect to carpenters was the prelude to his more striking interchangeability in respect to George **B.** Jashber, that most stirring of all the *dramatis personæ* he created for himself and out of himself. The great Jashber period, unlike the carpenters, however, did not come upon him spontaneously, full born out of a single emotion; George **B.** Jashber came on by fits and starts, as it were, developing slowly and irregularly, dropped altogether for days at a time, and then, returning to life, becoming at last so well conceived and complete a figure as to be powerful in the affairs of people whole decades older and more experienced than its creator.

The tall, half-filled sawdust box in the woodshed adjoining the now horseless stable was Penrod's studio,

his hermitage and his castle. Thither he retired when
life proved injurious and his world rigorous or scornful;in this soft-floored fastness he solaced himself with
dramatic imaginings of triumphant impossibilities
that should rend his parents or his sister or his
aunts or his teacher or Della, the cook, or others of
the ruling class, with convulsions of remorse, and
make lovely, amber-haired Marjorie Jones admire
him more than ever. Here, too, he kept a few private
articles that might have raised the rate of Mr. Schofield's insurance several thousand percent had their
nature been known to the agent who "wrote" the
policy. And yet these articles were so plain and un-
pretentious that Penrod had salvaged two of them
from a scrap-heap. These two were a damaged kero-
sene-can and an old chimneyless lantern. However,
after he had patched the leaks in each with sealing-
wax, both were practically serviceable, and the result
of what little dripping they did was absorbed by the
sawdust, so that no place in the box was ever really
uncomfortably damp to sit on. As for the rest of
Penrod's hidden store, it consisted of a varying supply
of corn-silk cigarettes, a few matches, a broken knife,
some pencil-stubs, an old cigar-box, an empty soap-
box and the secret manuscript of *Harold Ramorez*.

This last was an unfinished romance of road-agentry, kept buried beneath the surface of the sawdust and often forgotten for months at a time. Then it would be exhumed, perhaps on a day when Penrod was gloomy through some oppression, and several chapters —or, it might be, only part of a chapter, or no more than the beginning of a sentence—would be added.

The earlier portions of the narrative were concerned with the escapes of the handsome bandit, Harold Ramorez, from detectives and other vicious and inept enemies, including ghosts. and the reader (if a reader may be imagined for the manuscript) was led to place his sympathies entirely with Ramorez; for Penrod worked after the] manner of all child-of-nature authors, picturing his idealed self as the hero, which unconscious system, when followed with sufficient artlessness and a little craftsmanship, leads the child-of-nature reader to picture *his* idealed self as the hero, so that reader and author meet and fuse in the fiction, separating with reluctance at the end, yet consoled by the shared belief that the story was "good". Thus, although Penrod did not know that he had a method, he did have one; but, unfortunately, something happened to it—no infrequent disaster in cases like his.

He had what is sometimes defined in *argot* as a "change of heart", and it radically affected his hero at a high point in the narrative. Penrod began to admire detectives more than he admired bandits, and, although the author never realized what he had done, the too plastic Ramorez became the villain, while the hitherto malevolent but futile detective, Jashber, or Jasber, burst unexpectedly into noble bloom as the hero—this in the course of one chapter, short enough in the reading. However, in the writing of it Penrod consumed the greatest part of two mornings that were a full month apart, and, in the meantime, he had been to two matinées, had read several paper novels, and, moreover, had strained his young eyes at more than several unusually violent "movies". To be definite, this chapter was:

CHAPTER XIIII

HAROLD RAMOREZ decied he would go away from where was all such blodshed and plots of the scondrel Jashber so biding goodby to some of his freinds he got on the cars, he looked all around and cooly lit a cigrette.   Well said the conduter this is not the place where anybody is alowed to smoke and you have no tiket I guess I know that as well as anybody said our hero but you need not talk so much I got money and will pay $5 bill for a tiket

The conduter took hold of the $5 and put it in his

pocket. Then the conduter went on out Soon harold Ramorez had reached the city and he was just walkin arond
looking at the stores and houses and not hurting anything
when a shot rang out stratling our hero What could that be
said Harold I wonder why anybody would shoot at me
here where I do not know anybody bing Bing went the old
pistol bing bing bing it went bing bing

one hole went through our heros coat and one went in
his hat shightly crazing his scalp and porduc a flech wond
Harld smiled at this O said he a flech wond is nothing and
will soon heal up but I wold like to know what anybody is
shootin at me here for where I never came before in my
life and my emenies did not know I was going to any such a
place

O no they didn't O no not at all I guess said a tanting
voice O no it said

Harold whished to know who it was tanting him so he
looked around Soon he saw the foul Jashber still holding
the smoking revoler in his hands He was behind a tree
exept part of his face and the old pistol Well I would like
to know what did you have to come all the way here for
our hero said to him I was not doing anything to you and
you have no busines to go shooting at me said he I guess I
got some rights arond here

There folowed a deep curse Well go ahead and swear all
you want to because that will not hurt me but remeber
when you go to meet your maker each vile oth you say
now he will know about and probaly do somthing you will
not like

Well I will not stand this kind of talk said Jashber There
flowed a curse and some more vile oths I hate you Harold
Ramorez and I bet I get you yet said he

Our hero cooly tanted him for what he said then You

are the worst yet said Harold and you are double whatever you call me yes and I bet you wold not come half way

I will shoot you throgh and throgh said the scondrel you are a ——— ——— ——— ——— ——— (*The dashes are Penrod's.*)

Our hero smiled cooly at this No I am not any such thing said he but you are a double ——— ——— ——— ——— ——— because I just said so

Well I will not stand this said the scondrel He took a whistle out of his pocket and blew on it, there was another detective hiding behind some bushs and 4 more were also hid around there somwheres and all of a suden they jumped out

Soon our hero was fighting for his very life He had left all his wapons in the house when he came away on the cars He hardly knew what he better do so he took the foul Jasbers old pistol away from him and shot it off three of the scondrels went to meet their maker but now he did not have any more cartridges There was one scondrel left besides Jashber and these two scondrels bit him till thier teeth met in the flech makin flech wonds which he would soon get well from

He stabed the other one and now his emeny Jashber the detective was the only one left I guess your sorry you began it now said Ramorez Soon hunting around he found a long peice of rope and he fixed it arond the scondrels neck I am going to fix you sos you quit folling me when I go on the cars said he

The scondrel began to cry and our hero gave him a kick and tanted him O yes you wold folow me but I guess I'll show you this time said he

Jashber went on crying some more he got down on his knees and begged and begged but after all his persetcums Harold was not going to do anything such a scondrel so he fixed the rope the right way to hang poeple Soon he tied it up in the tree The scondrel holowed loud as he could but soon he was dead Soon Harold walked on off and fond a good place to sleep and made a fire to cook some bacon because he was tired now.

At this point, work upon the manuscript was interrupted, and not resumed until a Saturday morning four weeks later.

Soon after this some man came along and tacked up a sign that said $500000 reward paid to anybody for geting this crook Harold Ramorez put in the pentenartyry So Jashber the detective thougt he wold go upon the trail once more On the door of his ofice it read George B Jasber detective ofice on a sign because his first name was George B Well said George I would like to have $5000 Reward he is at his old tricks again and I better go after him Jashber the detective went on out of his ofice and the first thing he knew a young lady in an automobile wanted him to go with her so he got in and they went a long ways What do you want of me now that I have come out ridding with you said Jashber The young lady got to crying and all and took on Soon she said well I will tell you.

It is about the crooks is not your name George B Jashber the notted detective So George said yes he was and ask her what did she want of him besides Soon the young lady kept on crying and all and she said probaly he had heard the name of Harold Ramorez Yes I have heard the name of Harold Ramorez said George and he is a —— —— —— —— and I am after him because I will get a reward of $50000 for killin him How do you hapen to know the name of Harold Ramorez That scondrel has riuned the lifes of pretty near everybody

Well said this young lady now I will now tell you because my father is an old bank and Harold Ramorez has got this poor old man in his pouer sos he can get all the money that people have put in the bank and uless you will save my poor old father Harold Ramorez will proaly kill him and get the money and I will have to mary him If you will save this poor old man you can have the money and I will mary you

Soon they went in the house and the old bank said if George would save him he could mary the young lady and have the money himself Soon Harold Ramorez came in there because he had been looking through a hole in the cieling Yes sneered he you are a nice one coming arond here this way Ill just show you O no you dont sneered our Hero yes I will to sneered Harold and he began to shoot at George with his ottomatick Soon six more crooks ran on in because they had been lookin through the hole and wish to kill George B Jasber the notted detective but the young lady got a dager off the wall and pretty soon the old bank got killed by Harold Ramorez and Jashber killed the crooks by stabbing them in their abodmen

Look what you have been doing here sneered Ramorez and there folowed a deep curse You just wait said George and you will see what you get your vile oths are not doing me any harm and he went on and tanted some more with a smile

The scondrel called him names a while but George cooly lit a ciggrett and was going to put his arms over the young lady but soon Ramorez grabed her and pushed her out of a window where she fell in a mortarboat the rest of the crooks put there Soon Ramorez jumped after her and George had

to go on back to his ofice Soon a secert mesage came on the
wall like this it said this young lady was in the pouer of
the scondrel Harold Ramorez and the gang of crooks under
the east peir of the river Wenever our hero wish to know
about anything a secert mesage would come on the wall of
his ofice printed in large letters and then it would fad out
Sometimes it said different things and all such.

Jashber decied he would have to shadow some man he saw
when he looked out the window. He shadowed this crook
day and night till the scondrel went to the secret den of the
conterfiters under the east peir First he was shadowing the
crook night and day before he went to the den

George took some sailor cloths and put them on and
fixed himself all up sos nobody would know him in diguise
and when he got to the den the scondrel Harold Ramorez
was twising the young lady's arm and starting to whip her.
She was mad but she did not want to fight

Our hero told him he better not do any more like that
but the scondrel went on ahead pushing her all around
because he did not know it was Jashber the detective but
soon the scondrel had to go out a minute and George told
the young lady who he was Now I will tell you what we
better do said the detective Well what said the young lady
Well you put my sailor suit on and I will put yours on and
you can go on out and go to my ofce and when he comes
back he will think I am the young lady and try to whip me
but I am lots stronger than and he will see what he gets
So they changed thier clothes and the young lady went on
out because the crooks thought she was a sailor and she
went up to George B Jasbers ofice and sat there while our
hero was wating in the conterfiters den Soon the scondrel
Ramorez came back so he thought George was the young
lady and began again but soon Jashber got him down on

the floor and choked him till his hands met in the flech
Yes you try to whip me said he I could whip you any day
in the week because you are mistaken and I am not any
young lady

Well who are you you talk so much sneered Harold I
will show you who I am said he I am Jashber the detective
I guess you know who I am now Soon they were fightin for
thier very life Soon some more crooks came in and he had
to let him up and went on back to his ofice So ther the
young lady asked him if he arested Harold Ramorez

No I did not yet said our hero but I am going to the
next time because I want to have $500000 Reward.

So he put on some better clothes and they decided they
would go to a party that Harold Ramorez was going to be
at

CHAPTER XIIIII

THIS party was a party at some poeples house a band
was playing and all and soon our hero and the young
lady——

Here the manuscript was again buried beneath the
surface of the sawdust upon a peremptory summons
from the back porch, and Penrod repaired to the
house for lunch. He was thoughtful during the meal,
ate absently and did not return to the sawdust-box
afterward. Instead, he wandered about the yard for a
time, then sat upon the steps of the back porch, his
elbows on his knees, his cheeks in the palms of his
hands, and gazed unseeingly at the empty stable.

His thoughts were those that such a manuscript as

Harold Ramorez might be expected to stimulate in its producer; but they so far outran the speed of a writing hand that he had no desire to return to the composition. All his old ambitions had faded. He no longer cared to play the biggest horn in the band; no more did he picture himself in flashing uniform—not even as a general on a white horse. No; through tortuous adventures in his vivid mind's eye he wandered, cool, expressionless, resourceful, always turning up at the theatrical moment, shadowing male and female crooks night and day, a soft hat pulled low over steely eyes that nothing escaped, his coat collar pulled up to disguise the back of his head. A cigarette was ever ready to his hand (to be smoked for the purpose of concealing watchfulness of expression) and an automatic pistol always lay in his pocket (to be glanced at before he left his office or entered any door whatsoever). Yes; Penrod's childish ideals of circuses and bands and tinsel generals were now discarded pinchbeck indeed, ignominious and almost incredible. He had decided to be a detective.

So far as facts go—and they do not go very far at Penrod's age—he had never seen an actual detective; but he did not realize that. If you had asked him, he would have said that he had seen hundreds, and he would have been conscious of no untruth in the reply. In the theater, it was the day of "crooks" and detectives. Our plot-playwrights, being driven out of the "costume" centuries, yet being as ever dependent for thrill upon weapons, and the imminence of death and prison, had discovered with joy and gratitude that stage criminals can be made so virtuous in certain respects that audiences will love them, and wherever there is a criminal in a play, there must, of course, be a detective, sometimes many detectives. At this same time, there was a revival of detective plays—old-fashioned ones and new-fashioned ones, for many new kinds of detectives were invented. Not only upon the stage were detectives ubiquitous; many magazines ran overflowing with detectives; the Sunday newspapers were always an ounce or so heavier with detectives; they had daily serials about detectives; the bill-boards everywhere shouted with posters of detectives, and, above all, the "movies" filled the land, up and down, and sideways and across, with detectives and detectives and detectives—they could live no hour of the day or night without detectives. So what wonder that Penrod would have said he had seen great numbers of detectives?

And considering the nature of the most powerful

influences under which he came (at his age, those that affect the imagination being always the most powerful) it is not inconsiderably to his credit that he decided to be a detective and not a "crook". Perhaps —especially at the matinées—perhaps he wavered; for, on the stage, in many of these plays, the criminals were incomparably more attractive than the law-abiding people, who naturally must appear as persecutors and take the place formerly filled by villains in tan coats. But the "movies" (which nearly always punish or kill the "crooks") and the stories and plays wherein detectives were the heroes—these won the day, and Penrod's decision was upon the side of the law.

Now, as Penrod sat on the steps of the back porch, his imagined self—the Penrod in his mind—began to shift and alter. By the very act of writing (which is an act comparable to the changing of plaster-of-Paris from a plastic to a fixed state) Penrod had solidified his nebulous studies of the notted detective, George B. Jashber, into a fixed contour, and, by the same process, the more he thought of Jashber, the more he miraculously forgot himself. He became less and less conscious of the actual Penrod, and, when his far-away eye glanced downward, what it physically saw

—his knickerbockers and stockings and stubby shoes —bore no meaning. Penrod thought that he was wearing long trousers, rubber-soled shoes, a soft hat with the brim turned down, a long overcoat with the collar turned up, and that he had an automatic pistol in one of the outer pockets of that coat always ready to be taken forth and leveled at (or pressed against) a crook's abdomen. During this long, mystic sitting upon the back steps, the individuality of Penrod and the individuality of the notted detective were merging. Penrod was becoming George B. Jashber, or Jasber.

After a while he rose, glanced sharply over his shoulder, then, his right hand in the right pocket of his jacket, walked with affected carelessness as far as the door of the stable. Here he paused, looked right and left quickly, drew forth his hand from his pocket, glanced at it vigilantly, then, not in conscious imitation at all but by inspiration, gave the abrupt sag and heave to his shoulders of a "movie" actor about to make an exit. Penrod had not the slightest idea why he did this, and indeed, in the truest sense, it was not Penrod but George B. Jashber who did it. George B. having done it, Penrod passed determinedly into the stable.

He sat upon a box, facing the wheelbarrow; but the box was a swivel-chair and the wheelbarrow a large and polished desk, while the battered old door of the disused harness-closet gleamed mahogany and opaque glass with a sign upon it. This sign, in fact, became actual, for there was paint in a can in the woodshed, and the harness-closet door bore this rubric:

GEORGE B. JASHBER

DETECTIVE OFICE

WALK IN

VI

JASHBER DEVELOPS

IN HIS day-dreams and his night-dreams, more and more Penrod merged into the character of George B. Even when he played or romped in ordinary pastimes with comrade Sam Williams or the colored brethren who lived in the alley behind the stable, Herman and Verman, or with Roddy Bitts and Georgie Bassett, he did not entirely forget his new significance; there was about him the superiority of one possessing a fateful secret, and there were times, when (perhaps offended by some action of his playmates) he would mutter inaudibly, "I bet they better not do that if they knew who I was!" And once, his pretty sister Margaret overheard him communing with himself as he slowly dressed for school.

"Well, George, you got *your* eyes open all right? Yes, sir; I guess I have! Well, George, we got to watch out! Oh, we'll watch *out*, all right!"

Margaret laughed and called to him. "Who's George, Penrod?" she asked.

There was a silence, and then his voice came indistinctly, "Nothin'."

Now befell one of those coincidences in which life abounds, though we are beginning to be cynical about them when we see them on the stage or read of them in fiction. Thus it happened: Della, the cook, had an appanage of some vagueness, though definitely known as "Jarge". Jarge was a golden-haired, pale-eyed, strangely freckled young man, whose chin and Adam's apple knew but one difference, and that was merely geographical. On Sundays, Jarge wore a blue-satin tie, manufactured in the permanent estate of a tiny flat bow-knot, and, as the newspapers are so fond of pointing out, he wore more than this tie—but nothing else so noticeable. The tie and Jarge's chin and Adam's apple had a strong fascination for Penrod; he thought Jarge a remarkable person, and felt

avored by Jarge's conversations with him. Jarge
came for Della every Sunday afternoon and was not
infrequently to be discovered at other times, sitting
solemn and non-committal in the kitchen, when
some member of the Schofield family had occasion
to go there. To this family he was known, through
Della's reserved account of him, as "Jarge", simply;
and, as he was evidently much younger than Della,
he was accepted by the Schofields as her nephew—
or something; for so they alluded to him upon occasion.

Jarge was waiting on the back porch for his pre-
sumable aunt, on a fair Sunday afternoon in May,
when Penrod approached him and in a rather guarded
manner opened a conversation upon the subject of
detectives. Jarge proved congenial, and presently
informed Penrod that he, Jarge, himself, was a detective no less. However, he stated that the experience had proved disappointing and of no financial
benefit whatever. He added that for three dollars
anybody could be a detective. It was only necessary
to send three dollars to an address in Wisconsin, and
a badge, a certificate and a book of instructions
would be the certain result, unless the United States
mail-car ran off the track. Jarge had proved this to

be the fact, more than a year ago, by responding with three dollars to an advertisement; but now he wished he had his three dollars back. His gloom in the matter had anything but a discouraging effect on Penrod; on the contrary, an electric opportunity sparkled before him.

"Look here!" he said solemnly, his eyes grown abnormally large. "What'll you take for those things?"

Jarge had lost the book, and the certificate had been accidentally used by his landlady to start a fire in the stove; but he believed that the badge was some-where in his trunk. It passed into Penrod's possession the following Thursday evening, the exchange being thirty-five cents in the form of two dimes, two nickles and five pennies. Jarge had polished the badge for good measure, and it was as bright as quicksilver. It was shaped like an ornamental shield and bore in black intaglio the awing device:

MEM

GRAY BROS

PVT

DETEC AGCY

NO

103

From that moment, Penrod believed that he was Detective No. 103. That was as far as he went, and it was sufficient—the rest of the organization remained in his mind as something powerful behind a curtain of Wisconsin mist; it was enough for him that he was Detective No. 103. And yet, in spite of the fact that he did not at all question his official rank as Detective No. 103, he did not think of himself as Penrod Schofield, No. 103; he thought of himself as George B. Jashber—George B. Jashber, No. 103. None of his family saw the badge, and, for a time, neither did any of his comrades—not even Sam Williams. He wore it under his jacket, near his left armpit, and kept it beneath his pillow at night—to be handy, perhaps, in case of burglars.

There was one person, however, who was granted, not precisely a look at the portent but at least a glimpse of it. This was Marjorie Jones, and the glimpse came at the end of a short interview across Marjorie's picket fence, Penrod lingering upon the sidewalk there, in the course of a detour he made on his way home from school. He was so preoccupied —or, at least, he appeared to be so preoccupied—that Marjorie inquired about it.

"Penrod, what *is* the matter of you?" she cried.

"Well—" he said, neither removing the pucker in his forehead nor turning his watchful gaze to her. "Nothin'. Anyway, nothin' you could understand about."

"There is, too!" Marjorie insisted. "I believe you been havin' a fight with some boy and keep watchin, out maybe he'll come round the corner."

"Not," Penrod returned, relaxing no more than that.

"Well, what *is* the matter? You acted this way last time, too."

"Well, what of it?"

"I know you got sumpthing the matter of you, Penrod," she persisted. "I bet your mother's found out sumpthing you *did!*"

"She has not!"

"Well, then, you think she's goin' to."

"I do not!"

"I bet you do, too! I bet that's just it." And she began to sing an improvisation in a sweet, taunting voice:

"Penrod knows they'll ketch him yet.
Penrod's 'fraid what he will *get.*"

Thus mocked, he was sufficiently stung to abandon George B. Jashber for the moment and turn upon her in the true likeness of Penrod Schofield aggrieved. "You stop that, Marjorie!"

Marjorie felt encouraged to proceed with her successful treatment, seeing that it had dispersed his rather lofty preoccupation, so she chanted again:

> "Penrod knows they'll ketch him yet,
> So he's 'fraid what he will get.
> *Oh*, Penrod Schofield!"

"You *better* stop that, Marjorie!"

She leaned across the fence, laughing, and pointed at him with a clean little forefinger. "Why had I? Who'll make me, Mister Penrod Schofield? I'll sing it all I want to! I'm goin' to sing it all day! I'm goin' to sing it all night! I'm goin' to sing it from now till the Fourth o' July! Listen!

> "Penrod knows they'll get him yet,
> So he's 'fraid what——"

"All right!" said Penrod, and, turning a pathetic back upon her, began to walk away. But Marjorie checked her mockeries at that and called to him.

"Wait, Penrod! *Please* wait a minute!"

"Well, you goin' to quit?" he demanded, halting tentatively.

"Well, I *have* quit," she said. "Penrod, what *is* the matter of you?"

And as she leaned once more across the fence, her head close to his, he cast one quick, severe glance to the south down the street, and a second to the north up the street. Then, frowning, he said, "Will you cross your heart never to tell anybody long as you live?"

Marjorie was suddenly impressed; her lovely eyes widened. "Yes, I will!" she whispered, crossed herself, and stood waiting, breathless.

"Well—look here!"

Penrod flicked back the left lapel of his jacket, and Marjorie caught a glitter from near his armpit. He allowed time for no more than this glitter to reach her eye, but instantly flicked his jacket back into position, buttoned it, turned and immediately walked away. He walked rapidly and paid no attention to several appeals from Marjorie, who had but the vaguest idea of what she had seen and no conception whatever of its significance. A moment later, he had passed round the corner, never looking back and leaving her completely mystified.

She was not the only person whom his behavior amazed. Miss Spence, the teacher of his "room" at school, was pretty well hardened to Penrod; but his present developments gave her quite a turn. She would have been unobservant indeed had she seen nothing new in his eye; frequently she caught that eye bent upon her, or upon one and another of his fellow pupils, in the long, enigmatic looks full of undecipherable calculations. She noticed, too, that whenever he left the schoolroom he first became obviously furtive, heaved his shoulders as if about to do something desperate, and then departed with an odd intensity. He entered the room with the same intensity and, she got the impression, whenever he came in, that he had previously heaved his shoulders in the cloak-room. There was nothing technically contrary to her rules of discipline in these symptoms of his, and she found herself at a loss. He made her uncomfortable; but she did not know what to do about it, or even in just what terms she could speak to him about it.

Toward the closing days of the school-term (vacation now being at hand) Miss Spence found something to puzzle over that apparently had little connection with the part of her life concerned in her profession of teacher. She finally thought the matter serious enough to be mentioned, and one evening she spoke of it to a fellow boarder, a teacher in the same school.

"I'm sure I haven't imagined it, Miss Carter," she said, shaking her head. "I'm not that sort of a person. I didn't decide that there could be no other explanation until it had happened several times; but every evening I went out last week I had that curious and uncomfortable sensation of being followed."

"How awful!" said Miss Carter.

"At first, I didn't see anything or even hear anything," Miss Spence went on. "It was on my way to the eight-o'clock lecture, Monday evening of last week, and all at once I just got that feeling of someone following me. 'I'm being followed,' I said to myself—just like that. Then I decided it must be nonsense, and laughed at myself and went on. Well, you know I went to those lectures every night except Saturday of last week, and Tuesday, Thursday and Friday the same thing happened—and twice I distinctly heard steps behind me, and once I turned quickly and saw somebody jump behind a tree."

"What did you do?"

"I turned right round and walked back—and there was nobody there. He'd got away somehow."

"What did he look like?" Miss Carter asked eagerly.

"It was too dark to see much; I couldn't tell. Well, I went on to the lecture, and pretty soon I was sure he was behind me again, following me all the way."

"And when you came home from the lecture, did——"

"No," said Miss Spence. "That's the odd part of it. I never got the feeling at all, or heard or saw anything, on the way home from the lecture any of those nights, though, of course, coming home it was later, and you'd think if he was a criminal of any kind, then's when he would be around."

"But do you know of any enemy that would want to follow you?"

"I can't think of any enemy exactly."

"And what would they want to follow you for to a lecture?" Miss Carter cried. "It's the strangest thing I ever heard of!"

"I've thought back over all my family history and

everything I've ever done," said Miss Spence, "and I can think of only one person who could have any possible object in doing such a thing."

"Who is that?"

"It's a cousin of mine; his name is William Bote. He drank so much that nobody would speak to him, and finally he got to be sort of a tramp and disappeared. Well, my aunt Milly lives in this town, and she has a little property, and she is William's aunt, too. He might have heard somewhere that she's talked about leaving it to me, and he might have come here to try to do something about it; maybe——"

Miss Carter was an intuitive woman, instant in her decisions. "That's it!" she exclaimed. "If you can't think of anybody else it *could* be, why, of course it's this William What's-his-name——"

"William Bote."

"I'm *sure* it's this William Bote," Miss Carter declared. "A woman outside of an experience like this has more perspective than the woman who is actually having the experience; and I felt all the time you were talking that it was this Bote." She glanced at the clock. "It's a quarter to eight, and you say this was about the time he followed you all last week. Do you suppose he's somewhere out there now?"

"He might be."

"Let's find out," Miss Carter suggested.

"What!"

"Come on! Put on your hat, and go out alone. I'll wait two minutes and come after you, and, if he's following you, he'll be in between us. How large is he?"

"William? Oh, he was a little thin man, and very shaky."

"I'll grab him," said Miss Carter impulsively. "I'm not afraid. Let's hurry. Walk straight down the street and go slowly, and we'll show this William Bote that the age of terrorizing women has passed."

The two determined teachers proceeded at once to set the trap for Mr. Bote. Miss Spence left the house at a leisurely gait, and exactly two minutes later her friend set forth somewhat more rapidly. Before the latter had gone half of a block, she drew a sudden breath, partly nervous, partly triumphant, for in the near distance she perceived and identified Miss Spence, who was passing beneath a street-lamp, while between Miss Spence and herself a figure indistinctly yet undeniably flitted from one to another of the shade trees that lined the sidewalk. There was no question about it: Miss Spence *was* being followed!

Instantly Miss Carter determined upon her action. "Miss Spence! Cornelia Spence!" she shouted loudly. "We've *got* him!"

And she rushed forward while Miss Spence turned and ran back at full speed, and the mysterious stranger, thus waylaid and cut off between them, might have found himself a sudden prisoner if the mouth of an alley had not been opposite the tree where he lurked, and only about ten feet away. Both ladies screamed loudly as they saw a shadow streaking into this refuge; but both resolutely followed it at top speed and went shouting down the alley.

"Look!" cried Miss Carter. "I think he's climbing the fence!" And then, at a clatter of shoes scampering over wood, "He's got on top of this woodshed! I know he's up there!"

"He is!" Miss Spence rejoined. "I heard him! I can hear him now!"

The woodshed was a humble part of a property well known to both of them as the home of Samuel Williams, who was a pupil of Miss Carter's, and the two indomitable teachers, halting beside the shed, hammered upon its resonant outer wall—Miss Spence with an umbrella, which she had carried in lieu of weapons, and Miss Carter with a piece of brick she had discovered underfoot. Both also freely used their strong young voices.

"William!" Miss Spence shouted into the upper darkness. "William, you better come down from up there! You know we've got you!"

And Miss Carter went so far as to hurl her brick bat upon the roof of the shed. "You William Bote!" she cried fiercely. "We know you're up there! You might as well come down! We're going to have you *arrested!*"

Then both of them shrieked, for a flashlight first silhouetted the sky-line of the woodshed with light, and, rising, as its holder mounted the adjacent fence, illuminated the ominous roof, but disclosed only a vacant expanse of shingles.

"There's no one up there now," said a voice. Then an alley gate opened, and Mr. Williams and Mrs. Williams and Sam and two suddenly vociferous colored women appeared. Several people from neighboring houses, some pedestrians from the street, a small touring car and a patrolman likewise arrived, and shouts indicated that more were coming.

Penrod decided that he had made a mistake. As he crawled through an aperture in the farther line of Mr. Williams's fence, and made his way toward home as rapidly as possible, but painfully withal (on account of a gratuitous nail on the roof of Mr. Williams's woodshed) sounds of agitation and excitement came increasingly to his ears, indicating the beginnings of a neighborhood perturbation he had little anticipated; and, in spite of an almost unbearable anxiety to know who William Bote was, he felt that he would not do well to linger.

It became plain to him that he would have to give up shadowing Miss Spence. She was too excitable to serve as a Harold Ramorez; and George B. Jashber would have to find some other scondrel to shadow.

VII

JASHBER IS INTERRUPTED

THE days were longer now, and there was more time for detective work after school. Until Friday of the week after the fiasco, Penrod employed the daylight hours following the afternoon dismissal of school in shadowing schoolmates and acquaintances, and also practised this art during the earlier part of the evenings; but with results on the whole unsatisfactory and far from exciting. On Thursday evening, in the twilight after dinner, he did a little better; unperceived, he followed Sam Williams and Walter-John to a corner drugstore, and, peering through the window, made note of the fact that Sam purchased a bag of salted peanuts. When Sam came out, Penrod concealed himself from view, and again took up the trail, pursuing in silence, until Sam and Walter-John came almost to their own purlieus. Then Penrod made his presence known, stepping suddenly to his friend's side.

"You give me some o' those salted peanuts, Sam Williams!" he said commandingly. At the moment, Sam was not eating; the bag was in his pocket; therefore he was astonished.

"Where'd you come from? How'd you know I got peanuts?"

"Never mind," Penrod returned darkly. "I got ways o' knowin'. I know everything you do."

"You do not!"

"I'll prove it. You and Walter-John went over to Smith and Muhlbach's and bought a dime's worth o' salted peanuts. When they handed 'em to you you could hardly reach 'em because Walter-John was pullin' you the other way on account he wanted to smell at Smith and Muhlbach's cat, and she had her back all humped up and was fixin' to take a crack at him. You hand out that bag o' peanuts!"

Sam proffered the bag; Penrod helped himself, and there followed some moments of silence broken only by sounds of eating. "Well," Sam said, at length, "you might know that, but you don't know everything I do, because you couldn't."

"I do, too. I told you I got ways o' knowin' all about what anybody does I want to."

"All right then," Sam said challengingly. "You know so much, tell me what I ate for dinner and what my mother said to my father when he asked her when was my brother Robert goin' to get home from college this year. You just answer me that, you know so much!"

"I could if I wanted to; but that's sumpthing I wouldn't want to. I said I know everything about anybody I want to, because I got ways to find out— ways nobody else knows about."

"I bet you haven't! What are they?"

"You wait and see. Maybe I'll show you someday, Sam."

"When?"

"Well, maybe pretty soon." Penrod had become thoughtful. "Maybe to-morrow after school, and Saturday. I got to think it over, though; but I guess I will, Sam."

Sam seemed to be satisfied with this tentative promise, though not greatly excited by the prospect offered, and Penrod departed, ruminating. He had about made up his mind that George B. Jashber needed something of an organization behind him—subordinates, in fact, minor officials to be commanded, sent here and there, and set to trail criminals when George B. Jashber, himself, might be engaged with other matters, or perhaps preoccupied with duties at home. For such services, Sam Williams was easily available, and so were the two colored boys, Herman and Verman, who lived in the alley The idea appeared to be excellent, and, before falling to sleep that night, Penrod decided to begin the organization of his subordinate force on the following day after school. Unfortunately, however, the carrying out of this plan had to be postponed; an interruption occurred that even banished George B. Jashber, himself, for the time being, and, when Sam Williams made his appearance in the Schofields' back yard, the next afternoon, he had to be informed of unavoidable events indefinitely postponing the fulfillment of Penrod's promises.

Penrod sat gloomily upon the back steps with his elbows upon his knees and his cheeks supported by his hands, while not far away a bright-eyed little boy, nine years old, seemed to find pleasure in pulling Duke about by the collar, and otherwise annoying the patient little old dog.

"Watch me, Penrod!" the strange little boy shouted continually. "Look at me, Penrod! Look how I do with this crazy ole dog! Look how I do, Penrod!"

"It's my little cousin," Penrod explained sadly. "His name's Ronald Passloe, and he's here on a visit with his father, and he's an orphan or sumpthing, because he hasn't got any mother, and I haf to put in all my time with him. They didn't tell me anything about it until I got home from school. I don't know how long he's goin' to stay—maybe a week or sumpthing—and I got to be polite to him and everything all the time he's here. I already did take a walk with him, but that's all, and I s'pose I got to keep on hangin' around him. You want to go and get Walter-John and let him play with him a while, Sam?

Sam glanced again at Master Ronald Passloe, and evidently received an unfavorable impression. "Well, I guess not, Penrod. I guess what you were tellin' me about last night—how to find out everything you want to about anybody—I guess **you** couldn't——"

"No," Penrod said morosely. "I got to keep hangin' around him because he's my little cousin and visitin' us."

Sam looked once more at little Ronald; then he said, "Well, g'bye, Penrod," and went away.

"Hey, Penrod!" little Ronald cried, and, abandoning Duke, came running to his cousin. "Le'ss go in the lib'ary where papa is and make him give us the money to buy that little gun we saw in the drug-store window. C'mon!"

He dashed into the house, and Penrod followed more slowly, so that by the time he reached the door of the library little Ronald had already begun his pleadings.

"Papa, please," said little Ronald. "Please, please, please! Won'tcha, Papa, please? Please! Oh, please, Papa!"

"No; I will not," said Mr. Passloe, who was writing a letter at a desk by a window.

Penrod remained in the doorway and watched the beginning of a process never in his own case followed by pleasant results. But little Ronald kept at it.

"Papa," he resumed quietly, "it's only twenty-five cents. That's all we need."

"I don't care if it is," his father coldly returned. "Go out and play some more with Penrod. I'm busy writing. Don't bother me."

"But, Papa——"

"Go out and play, I tell you."

"But, Papa, how can we play when you won't give us anything we want to play with?"

"I don't care what you play with," said Mr. Passloe crossly. "I want to finish this letter. Go and play."

Ronald's tone became weary, but retained its affectation of patient reasonableness. "Papa, I've explained to you time and again——how can we play when we haven't got anything we like? And if you'd only just give me a quarter this once, I promise I'll never ask you for——"

"I won't do it. Didn't you hear me say I wouldn't?"

"Yes. But, Papa——'

"That's all there is to it! When I say a thing I mean it, and you might just as well not waste any more of my time. I've said I wouldn't, and I won't."

Ronald became more plaintive. "Papa, you don't

under*stand!* It's just a little squirt-gun that Penrod and I——"

"I don't allow you to play with any kind of a gun, and you know it."

"It isn't a gun, Papa. It makes just a little water come out of the end of it. It wouldn't hurt a flea. It's kind of useful, more than just to play with, Papa. Honest it is! If you were out walking or anything and had to have a drink of water, why, if you had this little gun with you, why, you could get a *good* drink out of it and be all right again. 'N' then, s'pose you were goin' along somewheres, and kind of looked around somewheres, and s'pose there was a house on fire somewheres, where some poor people lived, and they were all burning up or sumpthing, why, if I had my good little water-gun with me, I'd turn it on that ole fire——"

"Stop it!" Mr. Passloe commanded bitterly. "If you say one more word about that gun, I'll——"

"*Please*, Papa!"

"Not one single word!"

Ronald's manner and voice suddenly became passionate. "Papa, I *got* to get that little gun!" he cried.

"Well, you won't!"

"Papa! *Pop*-puh!"

"Be quiet!" Mr. Passloe shouted. "Be quiet!"

"Pop-*puh!*"

"You don't get it! No!"

"*Please!*"

Mr. Passloe uttered dismal sounds, and, having dropped his pen, massaged his hair with both hands. "If you're not out of this room before I count ten, I'll take you upstairs, myself, and put you to bed for the rest of the day! One—two——"

"Pop-*puh!*"

"Three—four—five——"

"Please! Oh, *please* let me get that little—oh!—gun." Ronald's voice was now syncopated with sobs. He seemed to suffer horribly. "Oh, Papa, you *know* how I want that little—oh!—gun! You *know* you do, Poppuh! You—oh!—*know* you do! Please, please, please, please——"

"Eight—nine—*ten!*" Mr. Passloe finished his counting with a great air of grimness, and Penrod gave Ronald up for lost. (He had long ago abandoned all hope of the squirt-gun.)

"There!" said Mr. Passloe. "I've counted the ten, and you know the consequences, Ronald. I told you what I'd do, and you deliberately——"

"I *haf* to have that little—oh!—gun!" sobbed

Ronald. "It wouldn't *hurt* you to give it to me, either! I'd like to know what—oh!—harm it'd ever do *you* just to let me get that little gun—oh! If I was *your* father and I had a boy that wanted a little—oh!— gun—I bet you'd think I was perty mean if I said— oh!—I wouldn't! The only reason you say you won't do it's because you don't *want* me to have a good time! You *don't* want me to! Please, please, please, *please!* PLEASE——"

"O Lord!" Then the dumfounded Penrod observed the hand of Mr. Passloe seeking a pocket. "Here! Hush! Be quiet! For heaven's sake go and *get* your little gun!"

Ronald, with no more words upon the matter, instantly grasped the resplendent coin emerging from that pocket, and the two boys departed, leaving the sacked parent murmurous behind closed doors. Briskly they went into the bright air, and lightly sped gateward.

"That was easy," said Ronald, in a businesslike tone.

Penrod looked with interest upon this type, hitherto unfamiliar to him. He said nothing, but stared at Ronald almost continuously as they walked along; and there was approbation in this gaze.

Ronald made several other allusions to his victory, downright contempt for his late adversary mingling with a little justifiable swagger. "Why, that was nothin' at all!" he said scornfully. "When *I* want anything, I *get* it!"

Meanwhile, the approbation in the eyes of Penrod increased in luster. However, it was somewhat dimmed by various occurrences after their return in possession of the squirt-gun. This implement proved even more fascinating in actual operation than in anticipation, especially as each of the boys wished to operate it while the other remained a spectator, and neither was willing to remain a spectator for an instant. But, for once, Penrod found himself hopelessly out-talked. Ronald claimed possession on the reasonable ground of ownership; he reminded Penrod severely of certain dogmas of etiquette concerning the treatment of visitors, citing many instances to establish his rights as a guest, and finally became so vociferous, as well as verbose, in a reminiscence covering the whole history of their relations to the squirt-gun that Penrod despairingly proposed a compromise somewhat to his own disadvantage.

"Well, what if it *was* your own father's money?"

he said. "What if you *did* see our good ole gun first
in the window? I was the one said I wished it was
ours first, wasn't I? And you got to use water in a
bucket out of *my* own father's hydrant, don't you?
Whose *bucket* is it, I'd like to know? I guess that
bucket belongs to my own father, doesn't it? I guess
this is my own father's yard, isn't it? Well, I got jus'
much right to use that gun any way I want to as you
have—and better, too! I guess you got sense enough
to see that, haven't you? Well, I tell you the way
we'll fix it. Each of us'll take turns ten minutes long,
and you can have the first turn. The one that's not
got the gun can stand in the kitchen doorway
where they can see the clock, and then, when the
ten minutes is up, I can come and get the gun, and
my turn'll begin."

Having thus spoken, he abandoned the hand-grip
that until then he had maintained upon the squirt-
gun as a sort of legal protest, and, turning his
back upon Ronald, sought the doorway, where he
came to a stand with his eyes conscientiously upon
the face of the clock.

Ronald capered over the yard, squirting flu-
ently. "Look, Penrod!" he shouted. "Watch me, Penrod! I got her workin' great now. Watch, Penrod!

I'm ole hose-reel Number Nine. Clang! Clang! Clang! Fire! Fire! Fire! *Git* that horness on them horses there, you men, you! Hurry up, now! Think I want to be all day gettin' to that fire? Click, click—horness, horness, horness!" He fastened imaginary buckles, and mounted to an imaginary seat. "All ready, boys! *Gallump, gallump, gallumpety—glump!*" Here, he not only gave this vocal imitation of a gallop but galloped simultaneously with his legs, contriving with his arms and shoulders the impersonation of a most passionate fireman in the act of driving, the squirt-gun now enacting the rôle of a whip. "Gong! Gong! Gong! *Hi*, there, you white horse, can't you keep up with that black horse o' mine! Go, you devils, go! Gallump! Gallump! Gallumpety-glump! *Whoa* there, you ole black horse, you! Here's the fire! Gimme that hose; I'll show you how *I* put fires out! *Fz-z-z-z-z!* That's the ole fire blazin' away. Look, Penrod! Watch me! *Listen*, Penrod! *Fz-z-z-z!* That's the fire, Penrod! Why don't you look? Look at the way I put houses out when they're on fire? *Fz-z-z-z!* Squirt! Squirt! Squirt! Pen-rod! What's the matter o' you? Whyn't you look see the way I'm puttin' this fire out? Looky here! *Fz-z-z-z-z*——"

At last Penrod looked. He had kept his eyes steadfastly, even sternly, upon the clock throughout the interminable period. "My turn!" And with an altered face, joy upon it, he ran and captured the squirt-gun from Ronald's clinging hands. "My turn now, Ronald! You go stand where you can see the clock!"

"I won't!" Ronald declared vehemently. "You gimme that little gun!"

"But it's my turn. We said we'd each keep it ten minutes for you and then ten minutes for me."

"I did not! You said so. I never said anything about it at all. You gimme my little gun! I——"

"I won't do it," said Penrod stoutly. "Not till you go look at the clock ten minutes. I looked at it ten minutes, didn't I?"

"You gimme my little gun!" Ronald insisted, growing visibly and audibly more intense. "It's my little gun, I guess! And whose quarter paid for it? You just answer me that, I'd like to ask!"

"I don't care who!" Penrod returned lightly. "Look, Ronald: I'm chief o' the Fire Department. This is the way I do!" And he began to romp over the grass with the replenished squirt-gun. "Watch, Ronald! Here's me!"

But Ronald showed even less interest in Penrod's performance than Penrod had shown in Ronald's, and, while Penrod—ever inspired to excel—now brought forth from his creative soul and painted upon the empty air not one mere hose-reel alone but the complex machineries of a completely equipped metropolitan Fire Department, including motor-driven ladder-trucks, chemical engines and something he called a "fire-tower", Ronald brooded near by with obvious malevolence.

He was not wholly unwatchful, however, as he proceeded to prove, about four minutes after the beginning of Penrod's "turn". The new fireman happened to be holding the squirt-gun somewhat loosely in his left hand, gesticulating for the moment with his right, and his back was toward Ronald. Ronald darted upon him, captured the squirt-gun with one swift and stealthy jerk, then sped away, laughing tauntingly.

"You give that back here!" Penrod cried, pursuing. "It ain't half a minute since my turn began! You never went near the clock! If I catch you, I'll——"

But Ronald was fleet. He disappeared round a

corner of the house, and Penrod beheld the squirt-gun no more that day. Ronald scrambled through an open window before his pursuer turned the corner, and, half an hour later, leaving the squirt-gun securely hidden within the house, the visitor again sought the back yard, discovering his host gloomily beginning the mastication of an apple.

"Biters!" Ronald immediately vociferated. "Biters! I got you, Penrod! Biters!"

"Yes, you will!" Penrod returned sardonically. "You got no more chance to get biters on this apple than———" But here he was forced to interrupt himself by a cry of sincere emotion. Ronald swooped upon him, this time in a frontal attack, and, with a motion as rapid as a prestidigitator's, snatched the apple from Penrod's hand. Again Ronald disappeared, cackling, round the corner of the house, safely in advance.

"All right for you!" Penrod called bitterly after him, abandoning the chase. "Go on; keep it! What I care! I know where's sumpthing better'n any ole apple, and just because you haf to go and act a pig, you don't get any what *I'm* goin' to get!"

Never was he less a true prophet. As he emerged from the kitchen, a few minutes later, triumphant, in the contemplation of half a dozen cookies, cajoled from Della and intended to be eaten tantalizingly in the presence of Ronald, this latter lay in wait behind the outward-swinging screen door, and again a surprise attack was successful. Ronald was one of those bright-eyed little boys who are as quick and as sly as cats.

Penrod was so deftly robbed of the six cookies that he remained staring incredulously at the crumby and still feebly gesticulating fingers of his left hand until a hastily massed portion of the ravished delicacies had already passed Ronald's esophagus and epiglottis and established itself as a through tourist for the whole route of his alimentary canal. The dazed eyes of Penrod lifted from his vacant hand and perceived the undulations of Ronald's slender throat as this journey was thus begun. Then Penrod made outcry and tried to retrieve what might be retrievable.

But Ronald had discovered that he was easily the fleeter. Disdaining to seek cover, this time, he dodged, ducked and zigzagged, eating spasmodically the while, and not failing to describe in rich words the ecstasies produced in his insides by the food, which he maddeningly affected to believe Penrod had

presented to him. He ate the cakes to the last in-
furiating crumb, dancing just beyond arm's length,
while Penrod formed a plan of retaliation, deciding
that he would obtain a fresh supply from Della, and,
behind a closed window, eat cookies at Ronald. He
went to the length of rehearsing mentally the scornful gestures to accompany this performance, which
might have proven an effective one if Della had been
a woman with a real heart in her bosom. Unfortunately, she was of those whom no pathos moves except their own, and for to-day she had founded
herself stonily upon the senseless and arbitrary
dogma, "Six is enough", her only variation being
quite as discouraging—"Well, annyway, you'll git
no more!"

Following this chilling siege, Penrod spent half
an hour, satisfying himself that when Della really
intended to hide a pan of cookies she was able to do it.
After this, he returned to the yard gloomily, but with
his hurt somewhat healed by time.

New injuries awaited him at the hands of Ronald.
The latter found it amusing to snatch things from
his cousin, and Penrod could not pick up a stick or
twig or even a pebble to throw, but Ronald made his
attempt upon it, and always (unless Penrod was

alertly upon his guard) successfully. By sunset, Penrod had begun to wear a badgered look.

He was silent, not to say heavy, at the evening meal; there was upon his youthful front something not unsuggestive of the careworn expression of Mr. Passloe, Ronald's father. And when Mrs. Schofield, with a mother's absent smile, asked her son if he and Ronald had enjoyed a "happy afternoon, playing together", Penrod's answer was naught. One would have said he did not hear.

Ronald, on the other hand, was talkative. He dominated the table—though Mr. Passloe frequently offered nervous protest—while the Schofield family (except Penrod) listened to the boyish chatter with the indulgent responsiveness that all polite people show to other people's children.

As Ronald talked on, disjointedly interrupting, squeaking, yipping, sometimes almost shouting, Penrod's parents and sister Margaret exhibited every token of friendly and approving interest. They wore the air of people greatly pleased by the conversation of a witty and distinguished person, and yet, all the while, little seemed plainer to Penrod than the fact that Ronald was, definitely, nothing but the freshest little smart Aleck on earth.

Penrod became, first, embittered; next, envious and
jealous; then he began to ponder, though dimly
Ronald's ways appeared to be successful. It might
pay to be like that!

This impression was confirmed during the service
of dessert. Ronald announced that he wished to
attend a "pitcher-show" that evening, and his
father promptly and sharply denied the consequent
application for funds. He denied permission as well,
concluding decidedly, "You'll be in bed before half
past eight, or I'll know the reason why!"

"But, Papa——"

"Not another word, Ronald. You can't go, and
we don't wish to hear anything more about it."

"But, Papa," Ronald persevered, "it's only ten
cents, and Penrod's papa will give *him* ten cents
and——"

"No, he won't," said Mr. Passloe.

"Well, then," Ronald responded briskly, "*I* don't
care if I haf to go alone."

"No; you can't go——"

"Well, then, you can give us twenty cents and
I'll buy a ticket for Penrod, too."

"Didn't you hear me say you couldn't go?"

"**Pop**-puh!"

"Not another word now!"

"*Please*, Papa!"

"I said——"

"Pop-*puh!*"

"I told you——"

At this point Ronald became emotional; his young voice quavered piteously. "Papa, it's *only* twenty cents! I should think you could spare *that* much when —you know what a nice time I and Penrod would have! Papa, I *got* to go to that pitcher-show! I *got* to!"

"Shame on you," said his father sternly, "making such a fuss at the table when you're on a visit! Look at Penrod, how nicely he sits and how quiet he keeps."

"Well, that's not so usual," Mr. Schofield felt called upon to say, coming to the rescue of Ronald. "Ronald seems to me a very nice little boy."

"I'm ashamed of him," said Mr. Passloe. "The idea of his making such a distur——"

"*Pop*-puh!" Ronald interrupted vehemently. "Pop-*puh!* You *got* to gimme that twenty cents! You got to *do* it!"

Here Mrs. Schofield attempted to mediate. She smilingly offered a compromise. "But dear," she said sweetly to Ronald, "if your papa doesn't want you to go this evening because it's dark and late—and I'd just a little rather Penrod didn't go, either— think what a nice time you can have to-morrow! When to-morrow comes, and all nice, bright sunshine——"

She continued to expand this theme, offering rewards and enticements—for the morrow. Even in the silent Penrod these evoked no responsive anticipations. A boy can look forward ecstatically to his birthday, to the Fourth of July, to Thanksgiving dinner and to Christmas. Those are the only morrows that weigh greatly with him, and grown people are seldom less intelligent than when they follow that eternal custom of theirs—offering boys beauteous morrows, invented on the spur of the moment, and easily recognizable as mere dismal words to offset immediate pleasures already within grasp. Ronald was moved by Mrs. Schofield's soft eloquence— moved to break out in a yell.

"*Rats!*" he vociferated, and set an exclamation point upon the shocking word—a heartrending sob. "Oh! I don't—*oh!*—want to go to any crazy ole

matinée to—oh!—to-morrow!" he wailed. "I want
to go to that pitcher-show *to-night!*"

"Ronald," his father warned him sharply, "you're
disgustingly rude!"

"Oh, no," said Mrs. Schofield lightly, "Ronald
didn't mean to be impolite at all. He's a very good
boy—aren't you, Ronald?"

Ronald paid no attention to her, renewing the
attack upon his father with vehemence. But the
murky glance of Penrod swept Mrs. Schofield; he
gave her a long look wherein strong injury mingled
with perplexity.

And why should he not have been injured and perplexed? To a boy, a visitor is a visitor for only the
first hour or so; after that, you know him about as
well as you know anybody. Penrod was unable to
perceive that his family was being indulgent toward
Ronald because the latter was a guest in the house,
and, if he had perceived this, the point of etiquette
involved would have seemed founded upon vicious
unreason; he could not understand why a guest
should be treated better than anybody else. But he
saw, all too plainly, that Ronald was behaving in a
way that would have insured punishment for Penrod Schofield—and here were Penrod's parents mak-

ing excuses for Ronald and calling him "good" and "nice"! Evidently they liked this sort of thing.

"*Pop*-puh!" screamed Ronald.

"One—two—three—four—" Mr. Passloe began ominously.

"Pop-*puh!* Oh, please, please, please, *please!* Papa, you *know* how I want to go to that pitcher-show! It wouldn't hurt *you* to let me go! What *harm* would it do you—unless you don't *want* me to have a nice time! Papa, you *don't* want me to! You *don't!* You *don't!* Oh, Pop-puh, *please, please!* PLEASE!"

His passion had become acute. Mr. Passloe groaned, "Oh, good heavens!" and plunged his hand into his pocket, drawing forth two dimes.

"C'm on, Penrod!" said Ronald briskly.

"Can I, Mamma?"

"Well—since Ronald wants to go so much," Mrs. Schofield said affably.

And, as the two boys passed out of the front door, Penrod happened to sneeze, and therefore drew forth his handkerchief; but before he had time to make it of any service to him, Ronald, with a malicious yell, snatched it out of his hand, and ran caroling down the walk and through the gateway— a sprightly soul with never a care in the world.

VIII

LITTLE RONALD

THIS snatching habit of Ronald's, jocular as it was, palled so heavily upon Penrod the next morning that he withdrew from his visitor's company, and, leaving Ronald the whole of the Schofields' yard as a playground, put several fences between himself and the snatcher, then emerged to the comforting, secluded alley, where he walked, inwardly communing. Ere long he encountered one Herman, who, in recognition of summer's approach, walked with brown feet bare and would go thus unshod until October. To-day his feet moved slowly

in the alley dust, for Herman was preoccupied with
a turtle, an intelligent animal about the size of the
palm of the brown hand upon which it rested.

"Yay!" shouted Penrod, his troubles forgotten.
"Where'd you get that turtle, Herman?"

"I trade him off'n Cubena Howliss," Herman replied.

"Who's Cubena Howliss?"

"Cubena live ovuh on canal bank," said Herman.
"She say, 'Look, what settin' right in pie-pan on
kitchum flo' las' night!' She say she mos' yell her
neck off. So she say she don' want him so *much*,
but she ain' goin' *give* no turkle away to nobody. I
trade him off'n her."

"What'd you trade?"

"I tuck an' give her a good piece o' kin'lin'-wood
an' a nice bode I foun' ovuh where's buil'n' a house,
an' a nice knife-blade."

Penrod touched the turtle's head, which had protruded from the shell adventurously. "Yay!" he
shouted. "A turtle's mighty smart, Herman. All you
got to do is just to touch 'em on the head or their
tail or one o' their feet or anything, and they'll stick
'em right back in again, unless you grab it and hold
on so's they can't."

"My goo'ness, you think I don' know that!" Herman exclaimed. "Whut I goin' *own* a turkle fer ef I don' know that much about 'em? Whut I want go an' han' ovuh 'at stick o' kin'lin'-wood an' 'at bode an' nice knife-blade to Cubena Howliss fer, ef I don' know no mo' 'bout a turkle 'n what you say I do?"

"I didn't say anything, Herman," Penrod protested. "What you goin' to do with him, Herman?"

"I'm go' to cut my 'nitials on his back, an' 'en I'm go' to put him in a bucket in ow woodshed an' wait fer him to grow. When he git big, my 'nitials go' to grow same as he do. Be two feet long some day!"

Penrod's eyes glowed and enlarged. The idea he had just absorbed was more than fascinating; it was compelling. "Look here, Herman," he said breathlessly. "Has this Cubena Howliss got any more turtles? Where's she live?"

"She ain' got no mo'," said Herman. "'Iss here turkle on'y one she own, an' she ain' got air' one lef'."

"My!" Penrod exclaimed. "I *would* like to own that turtle, Herman! What'll you trade for him?"

"Ain' go' trade fer him. I done trade to git him. Ain' go' trade to lose him."

"Why not?"

Herman was both obdurate and unenlightening; he seemed to love the sound of the words he had just uttered, and to consider them sufficient. "I done trade to git him," he repeated. "Ain' go' trade to lose him!"

"Aw, Herman!" Penrod remonstrated.

"I done trade to git him. Ain' go' trade to lose him!"

"How much'll you take?"

Herman plunged into calculations. "Well, suh, 'at nice bode uz wuff dime; 'at knife-blade wuff nickel— 'at's fifteem—an' 'at nice kin'lin'-wood uz wuff two cents easy. 'At's sevumteem. I take sevumteem cents fer 'iss here turkle."

"I'll buy him," said Penrod eagerly. "I'll give you the seventeen cents for him."

"You got 'at money?" Herman was surprised; perhaps a little skeptical.

"No; but I will have when papa comes home at noon. I can get him to give it to me." He smiled reassuringly—almost swaggeringly, in fact, and added, "Easy!"

"You kin?"

"Yes. And, look here, Herman: don't you go and cut your 'nitials on this turtle, Herman, because he'll be my turtle soon as I pay you for him, and I *d*on't want anybody else's 'nitials on any turtle of mine except my own 'nitials. You won't cut yours on him, will you?"

"Tell you whut I do," said Herman: "I wait till six o'clock, 's even'. 'F you pay me down 'at sevumteem cents 'fo 'six 'clock's even', he ain' go' to have nuff'm 'tall cut on him. You don' pay me down 'at sevumteem cents 'fo' no six 'clock's even', I'm go' to begin cuttin'. 'At's all 'a' way' I'm willin' to fix it."

"Oh, that's all right!" Penrod assured him. "I'll have that seventeen cents long before any ole six o'clock. Don't you worry!" And the contract thus comprehended by both the party of the first part and the party of the second part, Herman proceeded homeward with the property under consideration, while Penrod continued his walk in the alley. His spirits had risen decidedly. Already he felt the turtle to be virtually his own, and he had been convinced by the mere sight of it—in another boy's possession—that a turtle is the most delightful animal in the world. He wondered why he had never owned one before, and he determined never to be without one again.

His vision roamed the future; he saw the little

turtle growing year by year, the initials, **P. S.**, growing with him. He saw the turtle following him about the yard, large, docile, obedient. He would train the turtle to do tricks; the turtle and Duke and Walter-John (borrowed) would do tricks together. He would invite a large crowd—and Marjorie Jones —to a show in the stable. He saw himself as ringmaster coming forward with Duke and Walter-John upon one side of him and the turtle upon the other. "Laydeez and gentlemun, permit me to interodoos to your attainshon——" There was a warmth in his bosom as he walked. Already affection for this turtle was springing in the heart of Penrod Schofield.

A little before the hour for lunch, he slid over the back fence, and made his way into the house without being noticed by Ronald, who, squirt-gun in hand, was treacherously approaching Duke in the front yard. Penrod ascended to his father's room and found both his parents there, engaged in conversation.

"Papa," he began at once, "I'd like you to please give me seventeen cents."

"Would you?" Mr. Schofield returned unenthusiastically.

"Yes, Papa, please."

"That's a strange coincidence," said the father. "I've just been wishing some one would give me seventeen thousand dollars; but I don't believe anybody will."

"Papa, please give me seventeen cents."

"No, sir."

"Papa——"

Mrs. Schofield interrupted. "What do you want seventeen cents for?"

"To buy a turtle."

"A what?" Mr. Schofield inquired.

"That colored boy Herman's got the finest turtle I ever did see," Penrod explained. "He traded some good kindling-wood and a nice board and a nice knife-blade to Cubena Howliss for it, and the board was worth ten cents, and the knife-blade was worth five cents, and the wood was worth two cents, and that makes seventeen cents. He won't take a cent under seventeen cents for the turtle."

Mr. Schofield had begun to wear a look of irritation. "He won't?" he inquired dangerously.

"No, sir; and I do want that turtle."

"Well, you can't have it. It's time you learned you can't spend money idiotically, no matter how much or how little. You can find all the turtles **you** want, anyhow."

"I never did find a turtle in my life," Penrod asserted stoutly, "except one time at a picnic, and you made me put it back in the creek." His tone became more insistent. "Papa, *please* give me seventeen cents."

"No."

"Papa, it's the finest turtle I ever——"

"That's enough! You don't *need* a turtle! What on earth do you want a turtle for, anyhow? *We* don't want a nasty turtle around the house. You can't——"

"It could sleep in the stable," Penrod urged. "I'd fix a place for it. It wouldn't be any trouble or anything to *you*, Papa."

Mr. Schofield raised his voice. "Didn't I tell you you couldn't have it?"

But now Penrod's tone became almost excruciatingly plaintive. "Papa, *please* give me seventeen cents! That's all I want you to do. Can't you just give me seven*teen* cents?"

"No!"

"*Pop*-puh!"

"No!"

"Pop-*puh!*"

"Didn't you hear what I said?"

"Papa, please, please, *please*——"

Mr. Schofield sent a sharp glance at his wife, who had begun to look serious beyond her wont. "What's the matter with him?"

Before Mrs. Schofield could express an opinion, Penrod intervened. He uttered a sudden howl; a passion took possession of him. "*Pop*-puh!" he bleated. "I *got* to get that turtle! I *haf* to have seventeen cents! What harm would it do *you* for me to have that turtle? You don't *want* me to have a nice time with that turtle! You *don't!* Oh, Papa— oh!—Pop-*puh*—oh!—*please!* Please, please, please, *please*, PLEASE!"

Mr. Schofield rushed upon his son. By the shoulders he caught Penrod, and the latter found it impossible to continue his imitation, one all the more remarkable because it was only partially a conscious imitation. Most of it was instinctive.

His father shook him. "By George, he's caught it!" And he impelled the unfortunate Penrod toward a door that Mrs. Schofield sorrowfully opened, in response to a grim command from her husband. It was the door of a drear and dark closet, utterly without resources to aid an inmate in passing the time.

"You stay in there till you get over it!" Mr. Schofield said, as he closed this painful door. Then he turned to his wife. "By George, we want to cure him of *that*, right at the start! We don't want to be driven as crazy as poor cousin Henry."

Penrod was released by Mrs. Schofield subsequent to his father's departure after lunch. He was allowed to partake of some chilled remains of the meal but informed of a decree that he should curtail his activities until four o'clock; he was to stay indoors until that hour. Thereafter, he could go out; but not until the next day outside the yard. And upon this additional sentence, he spake not, yet his eyes were fierce and almost unbearable.

He underwent his penalties to the full, enigmatically looking out of windows most of the long, horrid time, his expression merely concentrating a little when across his field of vision Ronald went sweeping over the lawn, in further squirt-gun persecutions of Duke. But at eight seconds after four o'clock, Penrod threw open the rear doors of the stable and gazed earnestly at the abode of Herman across the alley.

"Yay, Herman!" Penrod shouted.

Herman appeared.

"Herman, I can't come out. I got to stay in our yard till to-morrow; but the stable's just the same as the yard. Where's that turtle?"

Herman's air was morbid; injuries lay heavy upon him. "You kin' keep 'at sevumteem cents," he said. "*Hain't* no turkle! I laid him down nice in dish-pan. Pappy sen' me to drug sto' to git him some 'at brain-medicine; mammy tuck 'at turkle an' frew him in ash-pile. Man come 'long; clean up ash-pile. Tuck an' tuck 'at turkle an' done ca'y him off! I tell mammy 'at's nice way treat sevumteem-cent turkle, a'n' she gone slosh me ovuh my haid wif' a dish-towel. Go on keep you' sevumteem cents; I ain' got no turkle!"

Penrod sighed. "I only wanted to look at him, anyway, Herman. I couldn't get the seventeen cents. I tried but—but I couldn't fix it."

"Well, mammy done fix my turkle," the colored boy said, withdrawing gloomily.

Penrod sighed again, closed the stable doors, and stood in the melancholy half-darkness of the carriage-house to ponder. Then a pleasant aroma came slenderly upon the air, warm and spicy, arousing some interest in the dejected boy; and he followed it to its source in the kitchen.

"G'wan away!" said Della. "Thim little cakes is f'r dinner, an' if yer pa eats 'em the way he use'ly does, th'r 'ain't more'n enough to go round."

"Oh, just one, Della!" Penrod pleaded. The little cakes were fat brown little cakes, not flat cookies. They were beautiful to look upon, exquisite to smell. "Can't I have just *one?*"

"If I give you wan, will you eat it an' g'wan away?"

"Honest!"

Della gave him one. "Well, keep yer word f'r wanst!" she said.

Penrod lifted the cake toward his mouth, and, as he did so, a yelp from Duke was heard outside the kitchen window, followed by the shrill triumphant cry of Ronald. Then, at this sound, reminder of the cause of all his woes, Penrod's hand, holding the cake, paused. A strange look came upon the face of Penrod.

"Well, if yer goin' to eat it, why don't you eat it an' g'wan away?" Della inquired.

"Guess I—I'll wait," Penrod muttered hastily, and, with the cake intact, walked quickly out of the kitchen and into the dining-room.

Here, engaged in a delicate semi-chemical operation, with the sideboard as laboratory, he remained not more than seven busy minutes, and when he issued forth the cake was still apparently intact; certainly he had not taken a bite of it. He went out into the yard and displayed himself before Ronald.

"Hey, Penrod!" cried the small visitor. "Watch me! I've learned how I can get Duke so mad with my little gun he almost bites himself!"

"I don't care anything about your ole gun," Penrod said languidly. "I got sumpthing better to think about."

"What you got?"

Penrod carelessly displayed the cake; in fact, his carelessness was incredible after the lessons Ronald had taught him. Penrod gazed absently skyward, opened his mouth, and, with thumb and forefinger, delicately lifted the cake toward the orifice.

Ronald's bright eyes emitted a purposeful gleam; he swooped like an arrow; his small hand shot out at Penrod's, and, in a flash, he had the cake and was away, his taunting cackle streaming behind him.

"I'll catch you this time!" Penrod shouted. "I been practising running, and I got you now. I'm goin' to take that cake away from you or break my neck!"

To settle this point and insure the latter alterna-
tive, Ronald, even in the act of ducking under Penrod's clumsily reaching arm, opened his mouth to its
capacity, plunged the whole cake therein and with
one great masticatory action attempted to swallow
the thing in the forceful manner of an anaconda.

He did not succeed. Instead, he uttered a dreadful cry; his eyes protruded, and, after a period of
terrible activity, he turned the squirt-gun straight
into his mouth and there discharged it. This seeming but to increase his distress, he rushed, bellowing, to the hydrant and ardently applied his mouth
thereto.

Showers of water sparkled up into the air, descending with rainbow effects lovely to the gaze of Penrod,
and, in the midst of this aquatic display, Ronald
contorted himself into grotesque shapes of protest,
squealing like some wild thing of the woods.

Greater suffering finally convinced him that water
was not the remedy for his ailment, and he tried great
drafts of air taken between heroic gasps. Then, relieved no more by air than by water, he gesticulated
insanely for a time and finally became coherent in
one vociferous word.

"*Pop*-PUH!"

He ran to the house, and the kitchen door slammed behind him; but still from the interior could be heard his searching appeals to his parent. Penrod stood listening for a few moments, while a better and a nobler expression shed a radiance upon his simple features; it was the look that comes to one who, after great turbulence, finds peace in his own soul. Nevertheless, there slowly penetrated an apprehension that the Authorities might consider that he had gone too far, and he sought seclusion in the disused hayloft of the stable.

He returned to the house unostentatiously at dusk, softly ascending by the rear stairs to his own room. But his mother had heard him, and she came in. The faded light of a western window revealed a small, meek form, sitting with folded hands.

"Ma'am?" he said gently.

"What on earth did you do to Ronald?"

"Nothing."

"He says you poisoned him. He came in screaming, and he wanted us to send for the doctor, but his papa wouldn't. Then he insisted on being put to bed. What did you *do* to him?"

"*I* didn't do anything."

"Penrod!" She spoke warningly.

"No'm; I didn't. I had a cake and I just put a spoonful of red pepper and a little tabasco in the middle of it, and——"

"And you gave such a horrible thing as that to——"

"No'm. He came and grabbed it away from me, and ate it up before I could stop him!"

Mrs. Schofield shook her head sorrowfully. "We knew it must have been pepper," she said. "Penrod, I don't know what your father means to do to you."

However, just at this moment, Mr. Passloe and Mr. Schofield passed through the hall. "I was looking out of the window," Penrod and his mother heard Mr. Passloe say, "and I saw Ronald snatch it out of Penrod's hand. Served him right; he has a disgusting trick of snatching. And anyhow, we'll have one meal in peace; he won't be down to dinner."

"Is he still suffering a little?" asked Mr. Schofield, and no one could have mistaken the hopefulness in his voice for anything else.

"Oh, I think he's convalescent."

There came a smothered laugh from each of these gentlemen; they seemed to be in the best of spirits, indeed. And then, as they were heard descending the stairs, Mrs. Schofield turned to Penrod with a last attempt to preserve her severity. "Penrod, you did a very dangerous thing to let poor little Ronald eat——"

"I *didn't* 'let' him."

"He's a very nice little boy," she said. "It was a shame!"

But a strange thing happened as she was speaking. Her words and her expression were at complete variance. The befogged Penrod saw this extraordinary contrast plainly, as she opened the door and the light from the hall fell upon her face. He perceived that she could not speak of poor little Ronald's sufferings without smiling.

IX

HERMAN MISSES A TREAT

THE next day at noon Penrod came home from church, accompanying his mother and sister, and walking sedately, pleased to be wearing an entirely new straw hat that was circled with a blue and white ribbon. Little Ronald sat between Mr. Passloe and Mr. Schofield upon the verandah and without apparent emotion watched the arrival of the small party from church; but after a moment he got up and quietly followed Penrod into the hall.

"Let me try on that new hat to see if it'd fit me?"

he said, in a tone almost respectful. "Will you, Penrod?"

"No, I will not," Penrod returned promptly, and, as he put the new hat upon the hall table, he added with severity, "You let that hat alone!"

"Of course, if you say so," the little cousin said, curiously meek. "Penrod, what's it mean out on that ole horness-closet in the stable where it's painted up 'George B. Jashber' and all that stuff?"

"Never mind! You 'tend to your own affairs."

"All right," Ronald said thoughtfully. "I guess you got the paint for it from those cans in the woodshed, didn't you, Penrod?"

"You 'tend to your own affairs!"

"I will. Did you know I and Papa are goin' away on the railroad train right after lunch, Penrod? I guess maybe after I'm gone away you'll be sorry you played that trick on me and made me sick yesterday, won't you, Penrod? Maybe sumpthing 'll happen that'll make you feel sorry about that." Then, as Penrod only stared at him, he turned toward the open front door, intending to rejoin his father and Mr. Schofield on the verandah; but paused. "Sumpthing *might* make you sorry, don't you think so, Cousin Penrod?"

He spoke so gently that Penrod almost felt a pang of remorse; Ronald's meekness perplexed him, and so did the little boy's well-behaved silence at luncheon. Afterward, when a taxicab came to take the visitors away, Ronald could not be found immediately and failed to respond even when impatient calls for him resounded through the house; however, he made his appearance rather suddenly, running from the back yard where he had gone, he said, "To say good-bye to Duke". Then, having expressed his farewells courteously to all the members of the Schofield family, he followed his father into the taxicab and drove away, with a final gesture that strikingly nullified the good impression he had just begun to make. Leaning from the open window of the taxicab, with his thumb to his nose and spread fingers wiggling, he tauntingly and insultingly squealed "Yah! Yah! Yah!" over and over until the vehicle passed out of hearing.

Something triumphant in this departing cry brought misgiving to the heart of his boy cousin, and Penrod remembered little Ronald's interest in the new straw hat. The hat was not upon the hall table where it had been left, nor did a search of the

house reveal its whereabouts; but Penrod had a
fatal premonition when he discovered Duke in the
back yard trying to remove a variegated coat of
paint by rolling himself passionately in the grass.
The new hat was in the woodshed, and only a glance
at it was needed to show that the paint upon Duke
had been little Ronald's mere afterthought. Penrod
lifted the wreck upon the point of a stick, carried it
round the house to the verandah where he found his
father and mother, lodged a formal but indignant
protest against the vandalism of the recent guest,
and received some sympathy. Then he returned
gloomily to the back yard, left the ruined hat in the
woodshed, and went to seek Sam Williams.

Sam was not at home, and Penrod returned by way
of the alley. Upon the doorstep of a humble cottage
that faced the Schofields' stable Herman sat sleepily, his eyes half closed, enjoying the strong sunshine of the afternoon. "Hey, whi' boy," he said in
a drowsy voice.

Penrod stopped for converse. "Where's Verman?"

"Verman way down in Tennasee. Mammy done
tuck an' gone way down to Tennasee 'cause Gran'-

mammy up an' tuck sick, an' Mammy gone to take keer of her an' tucken Verman along wif her."

"When's he comin' back?"

"Come back soon as Gran'mammy git well. What you want o' Verman?"

"Well——" Penrod said, and paused to frown importantly. "I kind of wanted both of you, maybe. I was thinkin' about tellin' you about it last week; but I had a little cousin visitin' me that made a lot o' trouble around here and's goin' to grow up to be proba'ly the worst crook in the United States, I expeck. Anyhow, I guess there's mighty few crooks that could behave any worse than he did. It was sumpthing like that I was goin' to tell you and Verman about, Herman."

"Like what? Like you havin' a mean li'l whi' boy come to visit you?"

"No. I mean about crooks. You know what they are, don't you, Herman? I mean if we got after one, f'r instance——"

"Where any?" Herman inquired, but without much interest, for he continued to be drowsy. "Where any we goin' to git after?"

Penrod scraped the dust with the side of his shoe. "Well, there wouldn't be any trouble about that if

I made up my mind to tell you and Verman about it when Verman comes back. This is the way it is, you see, Herman, about shadowin' crooks: I got to decide first what gang o' crooks we better go after; then maybe sometime I'll let you and Verman and Sam Williams maybe get on their trail or sumpthing when I'm busy."

Herman appeared to be too languid to make any response; one of his eyes had closed entirely and the drowsy lid hung low upon the other. He muttered indistinguishably; but, after a time, roused himself enough to make an inquiry. "Whut 'at l'il whi' boy done do to you?"

Penrod gave an account of the spitefulness of the recent visitor's final exploit. "I bet you never had anybody visit you that was as mean as that little Ronald," he said in conclusion. "I bet you never had any little cousin that painted a brand new hat and your dog, and then went away makin' that sign at you and your whole fam'y, the way he did!"

Herman roused himself a little more. "'At ain' nuff'm. Pappy tuck an' stay all night one time where my Uncle Ben live'. When night come Pappy tuck his coat an' pants an' stuck 'em under his haid to sleep on 'cause his pants had fo'teen dolluhs in 'em.

When he wake up nex' day he ain't got nuff'm under him but a bundle o' rags—coat an' pants an' fo'teen dolluhs done gone. 'Where my coat an' pants an' fo'teen dolluhs done gone?' he ast Uncle Ben. Uncle Ben say they done gone. 'I knows they gone,' Pappy say. 'Whut I wan' to know is where is they gone!' Uncle Ben say Oofus got 'em."

"Who?" Penrod asked, struck by this name. "Who was Oofus? Did he mean somebody named Rufus?"

"How I know?" Herman said. "All I know is Uncle Ben say Oofus done tuck an' come an' git 'em. He say Oofus done come an' tuck 'at coat an' pants an' fo'teen dolluhs while Pappy's sleepin', an' tuck an' gone outdoors an' buil' him a bonfire an' burn 'at coat an' pants an' fo'teen dolluhs all up. Pappy say, 'Where's 'em ashes? Where's 'em ashes?' Pappy say. Ef Oofus done tuck an' buil' him a bonfire an' burn my pants an' coat an' fo'teen dolluhs all up, where's 'em ashes?' Uncle Ben say Oofus done tuck an' scatter all 'em ashes. Uncle Ben say he len' Pappy pair of overalls to go home in. 'Tain' his fault, Uncle Ben say, 'cause he cain' he'p whut Oofus do."

Penrod felt that little Ronald's vandalism was outmatched by the misbehavior of Oofus; Herman seemed to have scored a point of superiority in possessing a relative more damaging than young Master Passloe. However, the point was not entirely settled in Herman's favor. "Listen, Herman, was Oofus your Uncle Ben's little boy?"

"How I know? Uncle Ben ain' say who Oofus is. All he say, 'Oofus done tuck an' buil' him a bonfire an' burn' 'em all up'."

"Well, then," Penrod returned, "he proba'ly wasn't your father's little cousin or else your Uncle Ben would of told him he was, so I guess that proves it, Herman."

"Prove whut?" Herman inquired sleepily, and now both his eyelids were closed. "Who prove whut?" he murmured.

"Your Uncle Ben would of told your father that Oofus was his little boy if he had been, wouldn't he? So that proves you haven't got any little cousin as bad as the one that's just been visitin' at our house. Oofus must of been a pretty mean person but he wasn't any relation to your father, or to you either, Herman." Penrod undoubtedly found a little solace in this thought; his voice took on the tone of one who triumphs in an argument. "It doesn't matter

how bad this Oofus was, Herman. I got the **worst**
little cousin in the world, and I bet I can prove **it**,
because Oofus wasn't your father's cousin, and
anyhow proba'ly your father's clothes were kind of
old. Oofus didn't ruin anything that was brand new,
the way Ronald ruined my hat, and Oofus didn't
cover a poor ole dog that couldn't help himself with
a lot of sticky paint and all different colors and everything. Besides, Oofus didn't make any sign at your
father with his thumb on his nose, and ride away in
a taxicab yelling 'Yah! Yah! Yah!' at him and all
his family, the way my little cousin Ronald did.
Oofus might of been a crook maybe, Herman; but
I bet he wouldn't of been very hard to manage if
your father had known how. That's what you haf
to know about managin' crooks, Herman; you haf
to know how to do it." Here Penrod became mysterious; he glanced up and down the alley, frowned
and passed his right hand over the left part of his
chest under his jacket. "Herman," he said confidentially, in a low voice, "I got a notion to show you
sumpthing, if you'll never tell. It's a secret; but it's
got sumpthing to do with what I was tellin' you about
a while ago. It's got sumpthing to do with what I
said maybe I'd tell you and Verman and Sam

Williams some day, if I decide to. I guess you'll be surprised, Herman; but I'll show it to you."

Again he glanced under a frowning brow to right and left, up and down the alley; then dramatically tossed back the left side of his jacket, exposing, for one moment only, the shield upon his breast, "Look, Herman!"

The effect was disappointing; Herman was not surprised, nor impressed, nor moved in any manner whatever. He was now sound asleep, a fact that slowly and somewhat chillingly became apparent. Penrod was disconcerted; the feeling he experienced was not wholly unlike that of an actor who finds himself minus an audience at a moment of crisis. He buttoned his jacket, scuffed dust again with the side of his shoe, and, oddly embarrassed, seemed to need to do or say something that would reduce a mortifying effect of anticlimax. He looked down darkly upon the unconscious figure on the doorstep.

"Huh!" he said grimly. "I guess it's a good thing for you I didn't let you see this badge, you old Herman you!"

Then, not quite sure what he meant by that threatening exit-speech, but nevertheless restored by it to a Jashberish frame of mind, he strode away, to fill in an hour of this long Sunday afternoon with a bath for Duke. "I guess you better not try to go to sleep while I'm talkin' to you," he said fiercely to the gayly colored little dog, as he drew him toward the necessary bucket of soapy water. "You hold still, you ole crook you!"

X

WAYS OF KNOWING THINGS

THE June-time moon hung over the town, and, in a wicker chair upon the ample front verandah of Mr. Schofield's house, a young man sat and sometimes struck little harmonies and chimes from the strings of a light guitar; sometimes, too, he sang to this accompaniment in an unobtrusive tenor voice, and at other times—and oftener—made as much love as she would permit to Mr. Schofield's pretty daughter. But in this he encountered difficulties that presently became part of a crisis.

"I can't and I won't," she said, after listening patiently to an appeal that would easily have reached those heights defined as "impassioned oratory", if it had not been delivered in a whisper. "It's just ridiculous, Robert. You've only had your Bachelor's degree three or four days, and next fall you've got to begin law school for three years, and after that you've got to go into somebody's office and wait to get a practice. I won't hear of such nonsense—not now."

"But why not?" Mr. Robert Williams urged huskily.

"Good gracious!" Margaret cried. "Haven't I just told you? It would be *absurd* for us to consider ourselves absolutely engaged. You ought to have your utter freedom."

"I?" he said, astonished. "*I* ought to? But I don't want to have my utter freedom!"

"Yes; you might," she returned gently. "You might see somebody else you wanted to marry, and you ought to be entirely free of all entanglements until you're established as a lawyer."

"But if I *should* see somebody else and wanted to marry her——"

"You see!" Margaret cried triumphantly. "You admit right away that you might!"

"I don't anything of the kind; I was just arguing. I was pointing out that if I got engaged to somebody else, as you say I ought to have the right to, I wouldn't be 'free' from entanglements, as you say I should be, until I'm an established lawyer."

"I never heard anything so mixed up," she declared.

"Neither did I," Robert returned, with some bitterness. "That's just what I'm trying to make clear. You say I ought to be free——"

"Of course you ought! At your age, a man just starting in the world, and with his way to make, ought not to have the burden of any obliga——"

"Well, what would I be asking you for, if it were a burden?"

"It's no use, Robert," she said firmly. "If I let you hamper yourself with this engagement now, I couldn't look your mother and father in the face, and I nearly always see both of them three or four times a day. I couldn't face them, knowing that I had allowed their only son——"

"Margaret!" he protested. "What *is* the matter with you? When I was home at Christmas you didn't talk through your hat like this."

"Well, perhaps not an only son," she admitted

placidly. "I just said that, and, besides, Sam's so
much younger he doesn't count. Anyhow, it can't
affect the truth of what I was saying. I simply
couldn't look your mother and father in the face if
I let you saddle yourself with——"

"Margaret!" he interrupted, in a voice of such
feeling that she paused to listen. "Margaret, you're
only making excuses for something you don't want
to confess—something in your own soul."

Margaret sat up straight in her chair. "I think,"
she said, with sudden frigidity, "I think when you
bring such charges against me, you had better explain
what you mean."

"Why, I wasn't bringing any charges," Robert
protested unhappily. "I only meant that last summer I thought you were pretty fond of me, and when
I came home for the holidays, you were so—so——"

"So what?" she inquired sharply. "What was I?"

"So—so friendly—that I thought we'd pretty well
settled things. And your letters, up to three weeks
ago, were—were the same way. Then you didn't
write any more——"

"I knew your time was occupied with commence-
ment."

"It wasn't," said Robert. "Not for three whole

weeks. Didn't I write to you—seven or eight *long* letters?"

"You should have been working on your thesis or something," she returned primly. "You shouldn't have been hampered——"

This word at such a juncture was too much for Robert. "Hampered!" he cried indignantly. "Margaret, how can you sit there and go on with such barefaced hypocrisy?"

"What!" she said. "'Hypocrisy?' Is that what you're charging me with?"

"You know it! You've changed toward me—that's the truth of it—and you're ashamed to admit it. You don't want to be engaged to me, and you put it on the score of *my* future, so you can take a high, altruistic ground, instead of confessing that there's somebody *else!*"

"What!"

"It's true! It's *you* who want to be free, for your own sake, not mine. I feared it; but I wouldn't believe it, not even when I was told so!"

"'Told so!'" she echoed sharply "Who told you?"

"I decline to state. But it's true. I was told yesterday that you'd gone everywhere for the last four or five weeks with a new man that's come here to live, named Dade."

"Mr. Dade!" Margaret cried angrily. "He has nothing whatever to do with it, and I wish you'd please leave Mr. Herbert Hamilton Dade out of this conversation. Besides that, I wish you would kindly use a little self-control—unless you *want* father and mother to overhear you inside the house. With all this fuss and excitement you're making, I should think you'd prefer that they didn't."

Robert dropped the guitar unheeded to the floor of the verandah as he rose in agitation. "It's true! I see it must be the truth!" he said; and he paced up and down, running his hands through his hair. "You never spoke in that tone to me before in your whole life! It *is* this Dade! And you sat there pretending you were thinking of *my* future, and that I oughtn't to be 'hampered'—oh, Margaret, I should think you'd be ashamed!"

"You—you are so unjust. I couldn't have believed —I couldn't—I——"

Robert, in his pacing, had reached the other end of the verandah; but, at this faltering in her voice, he turned, came rapidly back to her, and saw that her form was bowed to the arms of her chair and that her handkerchief was pressed upon her eyes by both trembling hands. She was weeping—weeping almost vehemently.

Stricken, the miserable young man threw himself upon his knees beside her, imploring. "*Margaret!* For God's sake, don't cry! I take it back! I didn't mean it! Don't! Don't! Oh, dearest, dearest, *please* don't!"

"You're so—so cruel!" she sobbed. "You—you have no right—it's not so. You mustn't call me 'dearest'—you said such awful things! There are times in every girl's life when she doesn't understand herself; but—but Mr. Dade hasn't been here since early in the week—he *was* here one evening—I admit it——"

Robert sprang to his feet. "You do!" he said harshly. "I thought so!" And he broke into bitter laughter. "Fool that I was!" he cried. "Yes; a fool in a fool's paradise, there at college—believing you *loved* me——"

"I never told you so," she protested. "You have no right to charge me with that, Robert!"

"No; you never told me in so many words. It was only the flirt's way to let a poor fool guess it for himself, while she never signs a document." And he struck the palm of his left hand a passionate blow with his clenched right fist. "Yes; it's only the old story of the flirt and one of her fools, one of her *playthings!*"

Moaning, Margaret lifted imploring hands, caught his arm and clung to it. "You *mustn't*, Robert!" she besought him, in a choked voice. "I can't bear it! You mustn't charge me with making playthings of men—you can't dream how miserable I am!" And the moonlight glinted on tears upon the anguished face she lifted to him. "I've told you"—she choked— "I've told you, Robert, that Mr. Dade *was* here Tuesday——"

At this moment there came an interruption that produced in both of these young people a condition of shock. A human voice spoke from just on the other side of a large Bath chair that stood against the verandah railing, about four feet away. "It wasn't either Tuesday," this voice said, in tones of warmest interest. "It was Wednesday he was here."

Margaret leaped to her feet. "Penrod!" she shrieked.

"What you want?" Penrod inquired, coming out from the shadow of the Bath chair.

"*How long have you been there?*"

"Well, just while you and Bob been talkin'," he replied casually, and continued, "I remember well as anything it was Wednesday and not Tuesday he was here, because Tuesday I and papa went to the movies and——"

But Margaret remained for no further introduction of corroborative evidence. "*Oh!*" she cried. With a tumultuous rush, she disappeared into the open front door.

"I guess she feels mad," Penrod said placidly, turning to Mr. Williams. "Well, anyway, I know I'm right," he continued, dropping comfortably into Margaret's chair. "I know I am, because I and papa——"

He paused as Mr. Williams, gathering up his guitar and a straw hat, seemed to be hardly more in a mood for conversation than Margaret had been.

"Well, you goin' home?" Penrod inquired, mildly surprised.

But the visitor only muttered something incoherent and descended the steps of the verandah.

Penrod hopped up and, quite unsolicited, accompanied him to the gate. "I know I'm right," he said, "because, after the movies, I and papa went to bring mamma from prayer-meeting Wednesday night, and, when we got back, that Dade was here, and Papa heard him call her a Princess or sumpthing and told her so at breakfast next morning until she got up and left the table. Well, after that—well, good-night."

Penrod added this farewell a little breathlessly, owing to the abruptness with which Robert swung out of the gate and closed it after him. Then the little brother watched the tall figure growing quickly dimmer under the shadow of the maple trees that lined the sidewalk; but, moved by a charitable impulse before it passed out of hearing, he leaned over the gate and called loudly, "He's around here all the time, anyway!"

After that, Penrod waited in silence, expecting the courtesy of a comment, or, at least, a brief expression of gratitude for his information—but nothing came.

XI

THE SCONDREL'S DEN

THIS lack of responsiveness on the part of one whom he felt to be fully his equal caused him some surprise, especially as complete cordiality had always existed between them; but, upon reflection, he decided that Margaret's conduct was responsible. Of course, Bob Williams's feelings were hurt by the way she switched into the house without saying good-night or anything.

Penrod had liked and admired Bob Williams faithfully, above all other suitors, for more than a year —in fact, ever since the preceding summer when Mr. Williams had given him a dollar, and the seeming curtness of this present departure caused no abatement in the liking and admiration. Besides, in the matter of Margaret, Penrod was firmly on Robert's side and even more firmly not on Mr. Dade's side. How a girl "with any sense" could hesitate between these two was a question he answered with too brotherly promptness—"Hasn't got a grain!" being his permanent decision.

However, she had influence inside the house, and he delayed before entering it, because he gloomily supposed she would be stirring up the authorities there against him, as she usually did when he happened to interrupt one of her conversations with a caller; and her manner had led him to conclude that she was more than ordinarily upset this time.

He was cheerfully surprised, therefore, upon repairing to the library, where his mother and father were engaged at cribbage, to be greeted casually, no reference whatever to Margaret being made. She had gone directly to her own room, and, as Penrod, in the character of George B. Jashber, presently discovered, she had locked her door and preserved a complete silence on the other side of it. Moreover, there gradually came to the great detective a sense of reassurance. He began vaguely to perceive that Margaret had no desire to make the episode of the evening known to her parents, and he was amply content with the mere fact of this reticence, which he did not feel it necessary to comprehend.

George B. Jashber was emphatically present at the Schofield family dinner-table the following evening, though the family and Mr. Herbert Hamilton Dade, a guest upon this occasion, were unconscious of the honor. Mrs. Schofield did indeed notice a peculiarity in her son's manner; but she misinterpreted it.

"Do your eyes hurt you, Penrod?" she whispered to him.

"No," he said. "Why?"

"You keep making that pucker in your forehead, I've noticed lately; and you keep looking out of your eyes sideways, as though it hurt you to look at anything straight in front of you. Does it?"

"No, it don't."

"Then don't do it, Penrod. You *will* injure your eyes, doing it so much."

"I won't either, Mamma."

"I don't know, but I think it might; I'm going to ask the doctor. What makes you do it, if they don't pain you?"

Penrod was annoyed. "Nothin'," he muttered.

After dinner, he disappeared (as was his summer privilege) until nine o'clock, his bedtime, and presently he was moving slowly on all fours along the latticework below the front verandah. Unfortunately for his mystic purposes, Margaret glanced down over the railing in the course of a little tour she appeared to be making to points of interest about the verandah.

"Don't play around here, Penrod," she said, and there was a businesslike tone in her voice. "You'll catch cold from the dew on the grass, and if you don't find something healthier to do, I'll have to call Mother."

Penrod made no audible reply, but rose and sauntered away. However, she seated herself on the railing, and glanced frequently over her shoulder, chatting gaily with Mr. Dade all the while, and George B. Jashber, after watching for some time this exhibition of a vigilance equal to his own, extricated himself noiselessly from a clump of lilac, entered the house by way of the kitchen, went up the back stairs, came down the front stairs, then, after a moment's debate, tiptoed through the hall and seated himself quietly upon the floor just outside the open door of the library. He had caught words from the two cribbage players that acutely interested him.

"Well, I'd just like to know who he *is*," Mr. Schofield was saying. "I don't like to have every Tom, Dick and Harry to dinner without knowing anything at all about them."

"But Mr. Dade seems to be a very pleasant young man," Mrs. Schofield said mildly. "He has nice manners——"

"'Manners'!" Mr. Schofield interrupted. "Anybody can have good manners. Why, I knew a horse-thief once that had beautiful manners."

A low vocal flutter, soprano, betokened Mrs. Schofield's amusement. "Mr. Dade isn't a horse-thief, I fancy," she murmured.

"There's something a little slick about him," her husband grumbled. "I'd like to know more about him if he's going on coming to the house this much."

"Why, Margaret met him at the church fair last month," Mrs. Schofield explained.

"Anybody can go to a church fair; that's wha they're for."

"But he knows *all* the girls of Margaret's set."

"Met 'em all at the church fair?"

Mrs. Schofield laughed again. "They're all excite about him, because he's so good-looking and differ ent. You're worse than Penrod. As soon as a youn man shows the slightest interest in Margaret, yo decide there's something queer about him. Mr. Dad has good manners; he dresses well; he's very good looking—in fact, he's handsome—and he's traveled because he speaks familiarly of every city in th country; but——"

"But we don't know," he took her up emphati cally, "what business he's in, where he comes from. or even where he stays in this town. He hasn't men tioned——"

"But he did! The last time he was here, he told me he came from Gosport, Illinois."

"Well, where does he live here in town?"

"I don't know."

"No," Mr. Schofield said grimly. "And what busi ness is he in?"

Mrs. Schofield, a little piqued, replied, with satire: "He didn't happen to mention that either, so suppose that leaves us no option. Probably you're right; he must be a professional horse-thief."

Naturally, she had little expectation that this remark would be accepted at its face value; but it was not the habit of George B. Jashber to take sarcasm into account, except when uttered in either a savage or a mocking tone of voice; and he forthwith came to the simple conclusion that both his parents suspected Mr. Herbert Hamilton Dade's business, or profession, to be that of stealing horses. This conclusion, coinciding with the trend of his own impressions, gave him a great moment. He rose in silence; his fingers stole to his jacket pocket and took therefrom a well-whittled object of wood—the sketchy likeness of an ottomatick. He returned it to his pocket, and, after the proper heave of his shoulders, moved silently toward the open front door.

He halted, hearing his name spoken from the verandah.

"You mean Penrod?" Margaret said.

"If that's what you call your little brother—yes."

"Why, no; I don't think he goes down town often. I think he plays around the neighborhood here, most of the time. Why?"

"I didn't know," Mr. Dade replied carelessly.

"It just struck me that I've run across him **down** town almost every time I go out lately. I wondered if your mother knew about it; that's all. I thought possibly she wouldn't want him to be——"

"She wouldn't," Margaret agreed decidedly. "I'll tell her about it. Of course, a child of his age shouldn't be wandering around down there among street-urchins and newsboys."

At this, Penrod's expression became so scornful, and continued in that contortion so long, that he was forced to relax it because his nose hurt him. Meantime, after a silence and some murmured words, the verandah was the scene of a departure.

Margaret spoke regretfully. "It's awfully mean of you to go so soon!"

And Mr. Dade replied airily from the foot of the steps: "Too bad! But I've got to be on long-distance at eight-thirty sharp, Princess."

"Telephoning to—to someone in another town?"

Mr. Dade had a rich voice and a rich laugh, musically barytone and perhaps a shade conscious; he protracted his laugh now, as if he heard it with some pleasure, himself. "It's only business—but important in spite of that, Princess."

She made a small exclamation, half smothered **but**

impatient; he laughed again, and then his voice came from near the gate. "Good-night! Good-night, Princess!"

Margaret came in, looking pink and perplexed and cross; but Penrod did not see her—nor did she see Penrod. He had slipped into an unlit room adjacent to the hall, had slid down from a window and was now crossing the front lawn, hot on the trail. Mr. Herbert Hamilton Dade had indeed become the bandit selected by George B. Jashber for a ruthless running to earth; but this was the first opportunity Penrod had found to shadow him except in the daytime, and daytime shadowing had so far failed to reveal (on account of Penrod's various engagements to lunch and dine at home) the whereabouts and nature of Mr. Dade's dwelling-place. George B. meant to discover the secret lodging of the scondrel this very night; and, not only that, but where he kept his stolen horses.

Mr. Herbert Hamilton Dade walked down the street, humming thoughtfully to himself and lightly swinging from a hand gloved in chamois a polished yellow cane that flashed streaks of high light as he passed the street-lamps. Surely no detective could have wished for a more easily shadowed scondrel,

and, since Mr. Dade not once glanced over his
shoulder to ascertain if he were followed, many of
George B. Jashber's precautions to avoid being
seen might have struck an observer as unnecessary

George B. took advantage, so to speak, of every
bit of cover; he flitted from the trunk of one shade
tree to the next; anon, stooping low, he darted into
the mouths of alleys and out again; several times he
threw himself full-length upon the grass-plots beside
the pavement and crawled a few feet before rising
and in these various alarums and excursions he cov
ered almost as much ground as if he had been an
inquisitive poodle out walking with his master.

Not less ingenious was he when the marts of the
town were reached. In this illuminated region he
sheltered himself among groups of citizens, or walked
behind strolling couples, or flattened himself in entry
ways, not forgetting to put frequently into practise
that detectivest of street devices, the affectation of
interest in a shop window; but never letting his eye
wander, for more than three or four seconds at a
time, from the flashing yellow walking-stick and the
yellow chamois glove that held it.

Proceeding in this manner, he traced the sinister

peregrinations of Herbert Hamilton Dade for more
than an hour. Mr. Dade went into a hotel lobby,
purchased a package of cigarettes at the news-stand
(as Penrod was able to observe from the entrance
to the lobby) and then spoke to the telephone operator. After this, he took a seat near by, and lit a cigarette and smoked it. Presently, the telephone operator
spoke to him in a low voice, and Mr. Dade went into
one of the booths. He remained therein for almost a
quarter of an hour and came out looking annoyed and
perspiring suspiciously. He gave the telephone operator a sum of money, left the hotel and crossed the street
to a drug store, where he purchased a glass (with spoon)
of soda-water, ice-cream and a flavouring sirup not
to be identified from outside the show-window. Then
he left the drug store, walked to the next corner
and stood there for several minutes, apparently
thinking. Suddenly, he decided to go on again,
and walked twice round the block with no object
discernible to Penrod, whose feet were beginning to
be painful. Yet he would not give up. He was determined to see this thing through to the end.

At last, he uttered a low exclamation—that is to
say, he uttered a moral exclamation in a low voice—

and quickened his pace; for Mr. Dade, having yawned audibly, had quickened his own pace and had turned into a dark and silent side street that led away from the main thoroughfare of the town. Before he had gone a dozen paces in this direction, he encountered a man whose lower features were wholly curtained behind a black beard, as easily supposed false as real, and both Mr. Dade and this bearded man came to a halt. Every word of their conversation was audible to George B. Jashber, who was sitting below the level of the pavement upon some steps leading down to a basement barber-shop.

"Well, good-evening," said the bearded man.

"Hello!" Mr. Dade returned.

"Any news?"

"Nothing in particular."

"Well, it's warm weather."

"Yes, it is," said Mr. Dade. "I'm going home to bed. Good-night."

And the other, passing onward, called back, in a voice not perceptibly muffled by his whiskers, "Well, good-night."

Breathlessly, Penrod waited until the black-bearded man was safely beyond the entrance to the barber's stairway; then he crept forth upon the pavement and once more took up the trail. Dade had distinctly said, "I'm going home to bed." Very well! George B. Jashber might have to defer to another occasion the discovery of where the stolen horses were kept; but at least he was certain of one thing: a short time—perhaps only a few minutes—would reveal the location of the scondrel's den. He was going there now!

Mr. Dade proceeded as far as the middle of the block; then he crossed the street and halted before a broad, arched doorway, rather dimly revealed by a faintly luminous globe above the arch. Then he opened the door, passed noiselessly into an entryway, and the door closed behind him.

Penrod darted across the street and marked the place well, the shape of the doorway and its distance from each corner. He was certain that he could easily find it again, either by night or in the daytime, as need might arise. George B. Jashber uttered sounds of satisfaction and quiet triumph; then, stepping backward into the street and lifting his eyes as he did so, became aware of a wooden sign above the globe. Here was a means of identification indeed! Four large letters were painted upon this sign, and, though the light was dim, the tired detective was able to discern them and to comprehend their meaning with absolute certainty. They were:

Y. M. C. A.

Unerringly, George B. had tracked Mr. Dade to his lair in the Young Men's Christian Association building.

XII

HERMAN AND VERMAN ARE ALLOWED TO JOIN

WHEN Penrod got home that evening, Mrs. Schofield was standing at the front gate, looking up and down the street in the darkness. For this reason, Penrod, having seen her before she saw him, quietly entered the yard by climbing over the side fence. Then he sauntered out of obscurity into the faint oblong of light that issued from the open door, thinly illumining his mother's anxious back as she leaned over the gate. He yawned casually, inquiring, "Whatch' doin' out here, Mamma?"

"Penrod!" She jumped, turning upon him sharply. "Where on earth have you been till this time of night?"

"What, Mamma?"

"Where have you been? Do you know it's after ten o'clock?"

"No'm," he said meekly. "I didn't think it was late."

"It's disgraceful, and your father's very angry. Where have you been?"

"Why, I haven't been anywhere, Mamma," he protested plaintively. "I—I haven't lifted my little finger, but you ack like I been doin' sumpthing wrong, and I haven't been doin' anything at all."

"*Where* were you?"

"Just playin'."

"With *whom* were you playing?"

"Why, just around," he responded, his tone aggrieved but reasonable.

"You weren't over at Sam Williams's," said Mrs. Schofield. "We telephoned, and Sam said he hadn't seen you at all."

"Mamma, I didn't say I was at Sam's, did I?" he

protested. "I don't see why you got to go and claim, all of a sudden, when I never said I was anywhere *near* Sam's, and go and say I'm telling a l——"

"Penrod, be quiet! I didn't say you were telling an untruth. I only said——"

"Well, it *looked* like it," he insisted accusingly. "I guess I can't lift my little finger around here but I got to go and get accused of sumpthing I never did except just lift my little finger. I expeck there's hardly any other boys around here their mother wouldn't let 'em lift their little finger without scolding 'em just because I lifted my little f——"

"Oh, stop talking about your little finger!" Mrs. Schofield cried, losing patience and conscious of a vague bafflement. "You march into the house and go straight up to bed. I don't know what your father's going to do to you. He's as upset as he can possibly be."

Upon this, Penrod entered the house with some natural hesitation, but was relieved to hear the sound of a shoe dropping upon the floor of his father's bedroom, Mr. Schofield being thus revealed as in process of disrobing for the night, and evidently not so wholly succumbed to agitation as his wife had indicated to their son. In fact, all that Penrod heard from him was a murmured question, a little later, and this came through an open transom over the closed door.

"Where'd he say he'd been?"

"Just playing in the neighborhood," Mrs. Schofield replied. "But it's dreadful, his staying out till after ten. It's no way for children to be brought up, and you *must* do something. I don't see how you can lie there and go to sleep so calmly when you know how worried I was over it."

Silence was the answer, though probably not intended as one, and, since nothing more was to be gained in that quarter, George B. Jashber, barefooted and in his nightgown, presently stole back to his own room and slid into bed.

In spite of some physical weariness, he did not at once fall asleep, but lay open-eyed, thinking exultantly. Probably a genuine, adult, official plain-clothes man, or detective, tracking a suspected person to residence in a Young Men's Christian Association might have felt rather discouraged, might have abandoned the trail altogether. Not so with the open mind of a boy. For Penrod, it was absolutely as easy to imagine a horse-thief having his lair in the Y. M. C. A. as anywhere else in the world. Why not?

And George B. would be hot upon the trail again to-morrow!

The difference between a man's way of thought, in such matters, and a boy's was exemplified at the lunch-table several days later, when Mr. Schofield once more dwelt grumpily upon the subject of Mr. Dade.

"Papa, you're just unreasonable!" Margaret protested, after a discussion that had brought evidence of some emotion into her voice and expression. "*Why* can't I go walking with him?"

"Because we don't know who he is."

"But he goes to everybody's house, and everyone likes him," Margaret said. "Why, he's been here to dinner in your own house, Papa!"

"Well, I didn't ask him," her father retorted.

"Papa, what's the matter with you? Why don't you like him?"

"I've told you."

"Well, what do you *want* to know about him?"

"I'd like to know one thing that I should think even you might consider *fairly* important," Mr. Schofield returned, with satire. "I'd like to know where he lives."

Margaret's eyes glowed sudden triumph. "He lives at the Y. M. C. A."

"What?"

"He lives at the Young Men's Christian Association," she said, laughing lightly.

"How do you know?"

"He told me the other evening that he'd taken rooms there, and he telephoned me from there this morning. I met him at the church bazaar, and he lives at the Young Men's Christian Association, Papa."

Mr. Schofield's expression, after a moment of incredulity, had become one of simple and unmanly disappointment. Margaret's, following an opposite course, now offered a charming contrast of liveliness.

"Is there anything more you want me to find out about him, Papa?"

The defeated man made no reply other than to eat morosely; whereupon his wife laughed aloud. "You can go for that walk, dear," she said to Margaret. "Papa's a funny man when he decides to take prejudices; but it looks as though he'd have to give this one up."

Mr. Schofield said nothing for a time; then he set his napkin beside his plate, rose, and, not looking

at his wife or daughter, uttered the reluctant words:
"Well, you may be right—for once."

Instantly they broke into peals of laughter, and
then, as he left the room, the happy and suffused
Margaret pointed across the table at her brother, and
shouted: "Look at Penrod!"

Penrod was worth looking at, though he was doing
nothing except with his countenance. However,
Mrs. Schofield found his action more disquieting than
amusing.

"Stop doing that with your face, Penrod!" she
exclaimed. "You'll ruin your eyes, and you'll be all
wrinkled before you're twenty years old. You *must*
get out of that habit; it's awful!"

Penrod, slightly discomfited, relaxed, and, breath-
ing heavily, left the table, followed by continued
admonitions from his mother and absurd mani-
festations of pleasure on the part of Margaret. Dis-
posing of these insulting sounds by closing a door
upon them, he went out to the office of George B.
Jashber's private detective agency in the carriage-
house of the horseless stable, and presently, seated
in the wheelbarrow, held an important conversation
with an imaginary client. He spoke in a low voice,
yet audibly.

"All right, missuz; you say your ole horse got stolen? All right, missuz; I bet I get him back for you in *no* time! Answer one question, please: Who was it stole him? I bet it was ole Dade, wasn't it? I thought so; I thought so! Pray take a seat, missuz. I got to get some o' my men up here." (Penrod used an imaginary telephone.) "Hello! Gimme number Two hundred and eighty-nine. Hello! Is that you, Bill? Bill, send Jim up to my office; I want him. We got a big case goin' on up here now, Bill." (He hung up the receiver, placed the stub of a lead-pencil in the corner of his mouth to serve as a cigar; then, rising, he rapped upon the wall of the harness-closet, listened attentively, rapped again, and returned to the wheelbarrow.) "That's Jim. He's one o' my best men. Come in, Jim. Jim, this lady here's mad at the Dade gang because they stole her horse and everything. We got to help her, Jim. You got your ottomatick with you, Jim? All right. Now, missuz, you go on down town with Jim to where it says Y. M. C. A. over the door, and you go on around in the alley that's behind there, and keep lookin' and lookin', and when your ole horse comes along, you tell Jim which one it is, and Jim'll grab him and make them give him up. Fifteen dollars, please. Good-day, missuz. Jim, come back here soon's you get the ole horse for her, because we got some more cases about the Dade gang, and I got to——"

Penrod paused abruptly; he started and rose to his feet, staring widely at the thin partition-wall of the harness-closet, while several small but lively chills twittered down his spine. From the invisible emptiness beyond that partition there had come sounds impossible for rats, cats, or dogs to make. Unmistakably, these sounds were of human construction; they consisted of muffled gaspings and of profound, irrepressible chokings—and they continued, becoming louder. Penrod stood it for perhaps eight seconds; then he nervously threw an old rake-handle at the wall of the harness-closet, and, uttering one loud cry of alarm, ran out into the yard.

Immediately arming himself with a clothes-prop, he returned as far as the open double doors of the carriage-house. "Hey, you!" he shouted, in a trembling voice. "You get out of our harness-closet, you ole tramp, you! You *better* get out o' there—my father's a policeman!"

The gasping and choking forthwith became a penetrating, silvery African giggle interrupted by sputterings and guffaws; whereupon Penrod, immensely reassured but enraged, entered the carriage-house and poked his clothes-prop savagely into the darkness of the harness-closet.

"You get out o' there, you ole niggers you!" he stormed. "I'll show you who you're laughin' at in there!"

Hysteric calls for mercy preceded the issuing-forth into the light of Herman and Verman. They were weak with laughter and in no condition to resist the clothes-prop.

"Lemme 'lone!" Herman begged, feebly defending himself. "Don' hit me no mo'—*please* don'! We 'uzn't doin' nothin' to you, Penrod. We'uz dess liss'-nun'!"

"Listenin' to what?" Penrod shouted fiercely.

"Liss'nun' to you," said Herman, who was forced to do all the explaining, as his very small brother, Verman, was unfortunately tongue-tied. "Me and Verman, we all time out in our alley hyuh you talk so much to youse'f ev'y time you come out in stable, we say, 'Whut 'at ole boy all time talkin' to hisse'f?' So whiles you in house eatin', we git in closet, an' when you c'mence talkin' so big wif 'iss here missuz an' Bill an' all 'at Dade talk, Verman went an' begin to

laugh an' cut up. Couldn' he'p it, 'cause you playin'
so funny!"

"'Playin'!'" Penrod echoed scornfully. "I guess
I'll show you that wasn't playin'! I guess if I told
you once what it was about, *your* ole eyes wouldn't
stick out! *Oh,* no!"

He frowned bitterly as he spoke; but Verman so
far lacked in impressionableness as to burst anew
into shrill laughter.

"Hey!" he shouted. "Hay hake a heek, mihhuh!"

Penrod correctly interpreted this as "Pray take a
seat, missuz", and the mockery was the more unbearable because Verman thought fit to illustrate
it by projecting his plaintively insignificant abdomen
and patting it pompously.

"Hay hake a heek, mihhuh!" he gurgled, and strut-
ted grotesquely; but his burlesquing ended in a
shriek, as the outraged Penrod, unable to bear further insult in patience, swung the clothes-prop in an
extensive semicircle that culminated at a point iden-
tical with a patch upon Verman's thin trousers.

"Oo hop ak!" Verman remonstrated.

"All right then," said Penrod. "You stop bein' so
smart about sumpthing you don't know what it's

about, then. I tell you, this is sumpthing perty danger's, and I guess you'd like to have a chance to get sumpthing to do with it if I was to let you, only I wouldn't."

"Whut 'at?" Herman asked. "Whut all 'iss here talk you makin'?"

"You see that?" Penrod demanded, pointing to the sign painted upon the harness-closet; and Herman and Verman examined with some interest the symbols of George B. Jashber's profession and location.

"Who is all 'iss here Jaspuh?" Herman inquired. "What all 'iss deteckatuff writin' mean? Whaibouts any Mist Jawge B. Jaspuh?"

"It's me," said Penrod simply.

"Who?"

"Me."

"Whut you talkin' about, whi' boy? *You* ain't no Mist' Jaspuh. You Penrod."

"I'll show you who I am!" Penrod retorted hotly. "You just looky here once, and I guess you'll see." And throwing back the breast of his jacket, he displayed, pinned near his left armpit, the little metal shield he had bought from Della's Jarge.

This time it was a triumph without any anticlimax whatever; the effect upon Herman and Verman was definite and complete in every way. In their altered attitudes, in their silence, in their almost protuberant eyes, they showed it. To them, such a badge was official; there was no denying such a thing. The contrast between the visible person of Penrod Schofield and their preconceived notions of a detective mattered nothing. This white boy, always a little mysterious, was unquestionably, unsuspectably Number One Hundred and Three. The glittering shield said so. Herman and Verman were overwhelmed.

"I guess you got gumption enough to know who I am now!" said the insufferable Penrod.

"Huccome—huccome all 'iss here?" Herman faltered. "Huccome it?"

"Hi!" Verman murmured faintly.

Penrod's expression at this moment was so profound that his mother could barely have borne it. "Looky here," he said slowly, "I'm shadowin' the Dade gang——"

"Whut 'at shad?" Herman asked.

"Shadowin'," Penrod explained impatiently. "It means followin' 'em around wherever they go, and —my goodness, haven't you ever been to a movie show, Herman?"

"Plenty!"

"Well, the Dade gang are the worst crooks there is, and I'm after 'em. You be Bill, Herman; and Verman, you can be Jim. I'll let you work for me, and I'll tell you all what to do, because you'll be my men. You must always call me 'George', or else 'Number Hunderd and Three'. Well, come ahead, Bill and Jim; we better start down town, because we——"

"'Down town'?" Herman echoed vaguely. "Wha' fo' we got to go on down town?"

"My goodness! We can't sit around here all day and shadow anybody, can we? I'll tell you what to do while we're walkin', won't I? We'll keep in the alleys all the way down, because we don't want anybody to know who my men are or about me bein' Number Hunderd and Three. Come on, Bill; come on, Jim! I guess we got a perty danger's job on our hands this time, men!"

Herman and Verman had joined, whether they knew it just at that time or not. Penrod and his badge swept them off their feet. And a moment later, the two smallish figures, and the third very small and raggedy one, might have been seen hurrying down the alley. Penrod talked continually in a low, important voice, and Herman and Verman listened with eagerness.

XIII

THE MAN WITH THE FALSE WHISKERS

IT WAS only a few days after this that Mr. Dade commented upon a singular phenomenon he had observed as a characteristic of life in that town. He and Margaret were sitting upon the steps of the verandah, enjoying the evening silence, when a curious hooting, somewhat like an owl's, came from some shrubberies in a corner of the fence. This sound was responded to by a melancholy but wholly undoglike series of barks out of other bushes more remote.

Mr. Dade made a gesture of discomfort. "What *is* that?" he said.

Margaret laughed. "Only Penrod and some boys, playing."

An odd voice issued from the fence corner. "Oh Mihhuh Habe hippum om hump hep!" it cried. "He hippum om hump hep hi mow!"

"What's that?" Mr. Dade asked nervously.

"It's only Verman," Margaret answered, laughing again.

"What!"

Margaret spelled the name. "He's a little tongue-tied darky boy," she added. "He lives in our alley."

"Well, that's curious," the visitor observed thoughtfully. "I've stumbled over a hundred colored boys down town in the last few days. It seems to me that the colored boys in this town have an actual habit of getting between people's feet; but the odd thing about it is that if I *have* stumbled over a hundred, at least fifty of 'em were tongue-tied."

As Mr. Dade's significant remark to Margaret amply indicates, Verman—otherwise "Jim" and later, "Number Hunderd and Five"—was of incomparable service to George B. Jashber. His value must be esteemed greater than Herman's, though the latter was both faithful and intelligent, for Verman's impediment of speech made him (to put his virtue in a word) probably the most efficient assistant detective that the world has seen. This defect of his, which he ever regarded less as a misfortune and more as a gift, made it possible for him to give secret information to his associates at any time, in the most public places, and in the loudest and frankest manner.

Thus, Verman called forth upon the night air: "Oh Mihhuh Habe hippum om hump hep! He hippum om hump hep hi mow," which Penrod and Herman, lurking out of sight of the shadowed person, were sufficiently familiar with the Vermanic cipher to interpret: "Ole Mister Dade sittin' on front steps! He sittin' on front steps right now!"

And when Mr. Dade would almost walk over Verman upon the threshold of the Young Men's Christian Association building, Verman, in the very act of extricating himself, would freely and loudly shout, "He hum howp!" or, "He hoe him!" whereupon Herman, posted within hearing, would relay the message to George B. Jashber round an alley corner: "He comin' out!" or, "He goin' in!"

Herman was the only person who understood

Verman at all readily, though Penrod, through fa-
miliarity, could at times decipher Verman's meaning
with fair results. However, George B. Jashber sometimes lost patience with his talented assistant during
the ceremony known to George B. and Jim and Bill
as "office". Penrod's continuing studies of detectives led direct to this institution. Penrod would
sit in the wheelbarrow in the carriage-house
with sheets of paper before him upon a box, and he
would frown and take notes while Herman and Verman "reported". Herman's report was usually simple
and uninspired; but Verman loved to talk. He found
his opportunity upon these occasions, and, with eye
dilating and gestures as unintelligible as his utterance, he would make a report that seldom failed to
shatter George B. Jashber's feeble power of en-
durance. Nor was his volubility checked by a mere
"That's plenty!" or, "Here, f'r heaven's sakes, can'
you quit?" Verman would go on, becoming shriller
and louder and happier all the while, until George B.
Jashber stamped the floor and rudely shouted, "Oh
shut *up !*"

When quiet (save for Verman's giggle) was restored, "What's he been talkin' about, Herman?"
Penrod would ask.

"Nuff'm. Dess all time say same fing he done say rs' time he say it."

Nevertheless, Penrod compiled and kept (usually 1 the sawdust box) something that stood for a record f the movements of Herbert Hamilton Dade; and his document, though fragmentary, must at least ave satisfied the typical movie and short-story letective who was its inspiration.

One morning, Penrod showed a recent page of the 'report" to Marjorie Jones, and, standing by, vatched her in his most sidelong manner as she read t. She read it aloud, of necessity slowly, and a little it too much in the tone of one conscientious over task at school.

"'Office'," she began. "'George B. Jashber. Report. Report of Bill and Jim. We got to catch this ook——'"

"Crook!"

"What is a crook, Penrod?" Marjorie asked, not profoundly interested.

"You go on readin'. You'll see."

Marjorie proceeded. "'We got to catch this cook'—crook, I mean—'and keep on the trall'—trail, I guess it means—'trail, night- and daytime. Jim report. The scoddel—scowendel—scondrel—the scon-

drel went to get his diner—dinner—at a place where
it says good meals seventy-five cents. Bill report
The scounderel talk to the crook with the false black
whick—whicksers——'"

"Whiskers! My goodness, Marjorie, don't you
know——"

"'Whiskers'," Marjorie went on, "'Whiskers
down in the barber stairs. George B. Jashber report
I was with Bill. The crooks said it was cool in the
barber and not much news the one with false wh—
whiskers said he got his hair cut. End of report'.'

"Hand it back!" Penrod said, and replaced the
report in the inner pocket of his jacket.

"What does it mean, Penrod?" Marjorie asked
politely, and, except for her politeness, her expression
inclined toward a vacancy that piqued George B.
Jashber. "Is it something you play all by yourself?"

This more sharply piqued him. "'Play!'" he
echoed morosely. "I guess if you knew sumpthing
about it, you wouldn't talk so much! It's a perty danger's biznuss."

"What like?" she inquired mildly.

"Well, you know what I showed you that day?"

"What day?"

Penrod jumped up from the grass where they were

sitting in Marjorie's yard. He began to walk toward the gate.

"All right!" she called after him. "If you want to go home mad, 'stead of telling me what it is, *I* don't care!"

Upon this, Penrod hesitated, halted, then came back and sat beside her again. "*You* know what I showed you," he said plaintively. "What makes you want to ack as if——"

"Honest, I don't, Penrod!" she assured him earnestly. "I don't remember any——"

"Well, look!" And he threw back his coat, displaying the glittering symbol of his chosen calling. This time, he allowed her a longer inspection.

"It's right pretty, Penrod," she said, and examined the inscription upon the shield with a little curiosity, though its significance was lost upon her, for she read the letters separately. "P, V, D, T, E, T, E, C, A, G, C, Y," she read slowly, and then her face brightened. "Oh, Penrod, I know what it is *now !* It's sumpthing like what they put in schoolbooks that say over it, P, R, E, F, A, C, E, and stands for 'Peter Rice eats fish and catches eels,' if you read it forward; and, if you read it backward, it means 'Eels catches alligators; Frank eats raw potaters'!"

"It don't anything o' the sort mean Pete Rice——"

"Oh, I didn't mean *yours* did!" Marjorie interrupted. "I only meant yours means sumpthing *like* that."

"It does not!"

"Well then, what *does* yours mean, Penrod?"

Penrod breathed hard. "It means sumpthing you wouldn't know what I was talkin' about if I was to tell you," he replied coldly. "I did tell you one thing and you never hardly noticed."

"What was it?"

"Chasin' these crooks. I told you it was a perty danger's biznuss."

"Penrod, you said you'd tell me what a crook is."

"Well——" He looked cautiously over his shoulder before proceeding. "A crook is—well, crooks are somebody that ought to be arrested. Anybody that's in jail is a crook, like horse-thieves and all. I'm after a gang of crooks now."

Marjorie seemed perplexed. "*You* are?"

"Yes, I am."

"What did they do to you, Penrod?"

"What?"

"What did they do to you to make you after
'm?"

"Well——" He paused. "Well, I'm after 'em all
ght, and they better look out."

"Who are they, Penrod? Is that little Carlie
'hitten one?"

Penrod was becoming exasperated by Marjorie's
pacity and her failure to be impressed. "No; 'that
ttle Carlie Chitten' is not one!" he said, bitterly
urlesquing her voice. "My goodness! I thought you
new anyways a little about sumpthing!"

"Well, why don't you tell me who these crooks are,
hen? Are they carpenters?"

"I'll tell you, all right!" said Penrod. "I guess
hen I tell you who it is, you won't talk so much
bout 'little Carlie Chitten' and carpenters so much!"

"Well then, why don't you go ahead and tell me?"

"Well, I will, if you'd ever give me the chance."

"Well, I'm givin' you the chance now. I won't say
thing till you're through."

"Well, one of 'em's a man that wears false black
vhiskers."

"You mean a grown-up man, Penrod?"

"'Course I mean a 'grown-up man'," said the

daring boy. "What do you think I'm talkin' about
He hangs around, and every little while he talks t
the other one. He's got false black whiskers. There'
two of 'em."

"You mean they both have false black whiskers
Penrod?"

"*No!* I didn't say they had, did I? *Who* said the
both—— My goodness! I said the one with fals
black whiskers had false black whiskers. I didn't sa
the other one had. He hasn't got any at all."

"Well, who is this other one, then, Penrod?"

"It's that ole Mr. Dade."

"Who?"

"It's that ole Dade comes to our house and sit
around so much."

"Penrod!" Marjorie cried, amazed. "Why, I know
him! He comes to see papa sometimes."

"Well, he's the crook."

Marjorie was utterly skeptical. "He is not!" she
cried. "Papa wouldn't let him if he was somebody
ought to be in jail. He wouldn't let him in our house
Penrod Schofield, you made all this up, yourself!"

"I did not!" Penrod cried, and he was sincerely
indignant. "That's just what crooks do. They go
around and get in people's houses, and then they stea

sumpthing or else get the people to sign some ole paper and grab everything they got. I don't care if ole Dade does come around and see your father, he's the worst crook there is."

"He is *not!*"

"He is, too! And perty soon he'll either steal sump-thing or he'll get your father and mother to sign some ole papers, and your father won't have a cent left to his name."

At last he began to make an impression. Marjorie showed signs of alarm. "Penrod!" she cried, her love-ly eyes widening, her pink lips parting.

"You'll see!"

"Penrod, do you think he'd steal papa's money?"

"I don't know," Penrod said modestly, "whether he'd slip it out of his pocket or get him to sign some ole papers, but he'll do *sumpthing* like that. Your father won't have a cent left to his name if he keeps on goin' with that ole Dade or the man with the false black whisk——"

Penrod paused, and his jaw dropped slightly in his amazement, a tribute to one of those supreme coinci-dences that happen to ordinary people only four or five times in their lives. Marjorie's father, **Mr. Paoli Jones**, was just entering the front gate, and by

his side walked the man with the false black whiskers.
Conversing seriously, the two passed along the path
from the front gate to the front door—and disappeared within the house.

"My goodness!" Penrod gasped.

"What's the matter?"

"That was *him !*"

"Who?" cried Marjorie. "Where was he?"

"With your father! Marjorie, that was the other
crook I and Herm—I and Bill and Jim are after. It's
the one with the false black whiskers!"

Marjorie's eyes flashed. "They are not!" she cried.
"You ought to be ashamed of yourself, Penrod
Schofield, telling such a story! They are not any such
a thing false! He had typhoid fever, and when he got
well, mamma coaxed him to let 'em stay on, on account of hiding his chin."

"Do you know who it *is*, Marjorie?"

"I should think maybe I *ought* to know him!" she
responded indignantly. "It's my Uncle Montgomery."

XIV

IMPRESSING MARJORIE

IT MAY not be denied that for the moment Penrod was taken aback. He rubbed his knee in silence, seeming to find an injury there; then, somewhat feebly, he inquired, "What's his last name?"

"Whose last name?" the offended Marjorie demanded. "Papa's?"

"No; I mean what's the man with the—I mean what's your uncle's last name?"

"Jones!" she replied, with an explosiveness beyond her years.

"Well," Penrod began uncomfortably, "well—all right."

"I guess it is *not* all right, either! You got to take back all you called my Uncle Montgomery or I'll never speak to you again."

Penrod felt desperate. He had come, that morning, to overwhelm Marjorie, to leave her almost prostrate with admiration and, conceivably, weeping with anxiety over the dangerous life his position in the world compelled him to lead. Here was a collapse indeed—just as he had begun to diagnose symptoms of success. Vaguely he sought some means to counteract malignant fortune.

"Well, I'll take it all back about your uncle."

"Every last word?"

"I will about *him*."

Marjorie looked at Penrod suspiciously. "Well, what won't you take every last word back about?"

"That ole Dade," Penrod said doggedly. "I won't take back *any* about him, because we're after him, and we're goin' to keep on after him—and he's a crook!"

"I don't believe it! I don't believe a word of it,

because look what you just said about my Uncle
Mont——"

"Marjorie," the goaded boy burst out, "didn't I
just *say* I took it back about your ole Uncle Montgomery? That hasn't got anything to do with the rest
of it, has it? I guess *your* eyes wouldn't stick out if I
just told you a few things about that ole Dade! Oh,
no!"

"Well, what about him, then, you know so much?"

"Well——"

"I won't believe a word of it unless you tell me!"

"Marjorie——"

"You don't know anything any more'n you did
about Uncle Montgomery. That's the reason you
won't tell."

"You listen here!" the incensed Penrod began.
"You just listen to me!"

"Well, I am listening."

"You listen, Marjorie! My father said this ole
Dade stole *horses*, and so did my mother, and I heard
them say it. I guess you ain't goin' to claim my father
and mother don't tell the truth, are you? Anybody
that calls my father and mother a liar——"

"Penrod! Did you *honestly* hear your father and
mother say that?"

"Yes, I did! And anybody that calls my father and moth——"

"Penrod!" Such passionate defense of his parents' reputation was not needed; they ranked as unquestionable authorities, and Marjorie accepted Mr. Herbert Hamilton Dade's status as that of a horse-thief. "Penrod, it's just terrible!" she cried.

"I know lots worse about him 'n that," he declared.

"Worse than stealing *horses*, Penrod?"

Penrod had carried his point; in spite of everything, he had succeeded in being as impressive as he had hoped to be. Nothing could have been more natural than that he should both protract and intensify the fragrant moment. Marjorie now seemed ready to believe whatever he said, and he more than half believed his ominous projections, himself. He became so mysterious that not only his mother, but a professional oculist, might have warned him to take care.

"Stealing horses isn't much to what *that* gang does—when they get started once," he said.

"Who's the others, Penrod?" Marjorie inquired, and, with gentle urgency, she added, "You took it back about Uncle Montgomery, Penrod."

"Well—he isn't; but they'll proba'ly get him to sign some ole papers or sumpthing."

Marjorie's eyes grew larger than ever. "Would they—would they make papa sign some, too, Penrod?"

"Well, that's just what I told you, isn't it? That's the way ole crooks do. First, he'll make your father sign the ole papers, and then proba'ly he'll want to get married to you or sumpthing——"

"Why, Penrod!" This was too far beyond Marjorie's horizon; she was not allowed to attend the "movies". "What are you talkin' about?" she exclaimed. "Anyway, I heard mamma say that Mr. Dade wanted to get married to your sister, Margaret."

"Well, I guess he does," Penrod admitted; and then, recovering himself, added scornfully, "I guess I know *that* much, don't I?"

"Well, you just said——"

"*Listen*, can't you, just a minute? Can't you listen just a *minute*? My goodness! If he got all your father's money and his house an' lot, then he could come and marry Margaret, couldn't he?"

"But you——"

"Well, he *could*, couldn't he?"

"*I* didn't say he couldn't, Penrod."

"Well, then, listen a minute, can't you? My good——"

"I *am* listening!" Marjorie felt that there had been a definite inconsistency in Penrod's statement; but, in a moment or two, as he went on, the inconsistency lost its definiteness, became vague, and then she forgot it altogether—and so did Penrod.

"This is the way ole Dade does, Marjorie. First, he gets somebody that drinks, or sumpthing, and gets him to help make some ole father write his name on the ole papers and then he proba'ly gets him arrested and put in jail, or else he takes and kills him——"

"Which one, Penrod? Which one does he kill?"

He deliberated. "Well, gener'ly the one that drinks, and then he takes all the other one's money and his house an' lot. Well, f'r instance, supposin' your Uncle Montgomery is the one that drinks——"

"He does not! He doesn't either drink, and you shan't say——"

"Well, I didn't say he *did*, did I? My goodness, I just said—well, even if he don't drink or anything, I bet ole Dade'll make your father give him all his money and his house an' lot and everything, and *then* where'll you be?"

Marjorie was disturbed, but she had a reassuring thought. "Papa wouldn't do it. He wouldn't give Uncle Montgomery——"

"I didn't say he'd give it to your uncle. He'd haf to give it to ole Dade. My goodness!"

"Why, papa wouldn't give it to Mr. Dade! If he wouldn't give it to Uncle Montgomery, he wouldn't take and give it to——"

"You'll see!"

"Well, I don't *think* he would, Penrod."

"Listen here, Marjorie," Penrod said argumentatively. "You don't know as much as I do, do you?"

"Well, I know any way almost as much," Marjorie returned stoutly.

"Well, almost as much isn't as much," said Penrod. "And you don't know *half* what I know about crooks. You don't know anything at all about 'em, and I know 'most everything."

"Well, what of it?"

"Well," said Penrod, "you better look out, that's all; and your father better look out, or, first thing he knows, there'll be—there'll be lots o' trouble around here!"

His manner (that of one knowing much more than circumstances permitted him to tell) had a powerful effect upon Marjorie, who was becoming seriously alarmed. "Why, papa would go and get that bad man arrested!" she said, but without strong conviction, for it had begun to seem to her that her father was in the toils. However, she had another hopeful thought: "He'd rather have him arrested, any day, than give him his house an' lot."

Penrod had no verbal reply for this; yet he had talked himself into the belief that Mr. Jones was somehow inextricably ensnared by the crook, Dade, and Marjorie's reasonable idea failed to shake him. He made some sounds of derision, and then shook his head portentously.

"Well, he would, wouldn't he?" Marjorie urged. "*Why* wouldn't he?"

"You just wait and see, Marjorie Jones!" said Penrod gloomily.

Marjorie's face fell; again all seemed lost. "Are you *sure*, Penrod?" she quavered.

"You just wait and see."

"Pen——" She paused, interrupted by a call from the house.

"Lunch, Marjorie! Come to the table!"

"I'm coming, Mamma." She took a few steps toward Penrod, who was already moving in the direction of the front gate. "Penrod, do you think——"

"You just wait and see, Marjorie Jones!"

"Oh, Penrod, please——"

In spite of her appealing voice, he continued upon his way; and the summons from the house was repeated.

"Marjorie!"

Thereupon, Marjorie turned obediently and went into the house. Meanwhile, a feeling, undeniably to be diagnosed as one of satisfaction, became part of Penrod's genuinely ominous forebodings on behalf of the Jones family; he was justifiably confident that Marjorie regarded him as an important person not immeasurably unlike an actual George B. Jashber. Still, he had another feeling underneath his satisfaction and his foreboding. This third feeling was less active and feebler than the two others—but it was there. And if he could have seen the excitement in Marjorie's face as she went in to lunch with her family and her Uncle Montgomery, and if he could have read her impulses under that excitement, this relatively insignificant third feeling would certainly have become, upon the instant, the most powerful one of the three.

It consisted of a shimmering disquiet, a foggy sense of having dabbled in vast matters, of having done something—somehow—somewhere—that might bring about results upon the adult plane and far out of his range and class. It did not last long, but while it was present within him, Penrod felt a little uncomfortable.

XV

THE PURSUIT OF DADE

THAT afternoon Sam Williams returned from a visit to his uncle's farm where he had happily spent the fortnight elapsed since the beginning of the summer vacation. He had heard something there that gave him an exciting new idea for the future career of Walter-John, and, taking that still cumbersome pup with him upon a leash, he sought out his friend Penrod, thus walking straight into the arms of another of those coincidences that attend upon the adventures of people engaged in the discovery of crime and the detection of criminals. He came upon Penrod, Herman and Verman, as the three sat making up the day's Report in the Jashberian office, though of course Sam was unaware of what thus preoccupied them, and even that they were in an office at all. He greeted them cheerfully, and, not realizing that he was intruding, began at once to explain his new idea.

"Look, Penrod!" he said. "Listen! I know sumpthing I bet you don't know, or even Herman and Verman, either. John Carmichael told me out on my uncle's farm where I been, and I bet none of you know anything at all about it."

"Never mind," Penrod said coldly. "We're kind o' busy now, Sam. Maybe I'll tell you sumpthing about it some day; but not now, because Herman and Verman and I got a good deal on our hands to-day. If you want to play some game or sumpthing you better go find Georgie Bassett or Roddy Bitts or——"

"I don't either want to play any ole game or anything," Sam returned, aggrieved. "John Carmichael told me sumpthing out at my uncle's farm, and I'm goin' to train my good ole dog to do it. When I get him trained I guess you won't feel sick you never trained Duke like that or anything! Oh, no! I guess and John won't make you and Duke look cheap or anything! You won't come around then and say, 'Why didn't you tell me about it so I could train my dog that way, too, Sam?' Oh, no!"

"What way?" Penrod asked scornfully. "What way would I waste all my good time and everything wantin' to train Duke to jump through a hoop or sumpthing you're talkin' so much about. What way?"

"'Jump through a hoop'!" Sam exclaimed decisively. "This dog o' mine isn't goin' to waste any time like that any more'n you would. You wait and see! Some day you'll see me just give John Carmichael, here, one sniff of some ole crook's shoe or his pocket-book or sumpthing, and then—oh, my! Go it, you bloodhound you!"

"What you talkin' about?"

"Listen!" Sam said. "John Carmichael told me that over at the county-seat, near where my uncle's farm is, the sheriff keeps a couple o' bloodhounds. If some ole crook gets out o' jail there or anything, they let the bloodhounds smell sumpthing that belonged to him, like his shoes or his hat or anything, and then—Whizz! those two bloodhounds go after him and catch him and pull him down! That's just what John Carmichael said; they pull him down, John said, and then they hold him there till the sheriff comes and arrests him again. John Carmichael said there was proba'ly some bloodhound in John Carmichael, and anyhow lots of other kinds o' dogs besides bloodhounds could be trained to go after crooks just the same as bloodhounds do. So proba'ly Duke could be trained to do it, 'specially if we trained him along with John Carmichael. John Carmichael said he was almost sure John Carmichael had proba'ly a whole lot o' bloodhound in him, and John Carmichael said John would learn how without any trouble at all, so if you want to——"

"Hol' on a minute!" It was Herman who interrupted; he looked interested but puzzled. "Whut is all 'iss here John Cowmikles? You say John Cowmikles say John Cowmikles got bloodhoun' in him, an' you go on talk so all mixed up about how John Cowmikles say John Cowmikles say John Cowmikles got bloodhoun' in him——"

"It isn't mixed up at all," Sam interrupted crossly. "John Carmichael works on my uncle's farm, and he's the man that gave me John Carmichael, and he said I could train John Carmichael——"

"Hol' on a minute! My goo'niss! John Cowmikles tell you——"

"There's two of 'em," Sam explained. "What's the matter of you, Herman? Can't you understand anything at all? Look! This dog is named John Carmichael because I named him for the other one that gave him to me. The one on the farm is a man, but this one is a dog, and both their names are John Carmichael. The man on the farm that's named John Carmichael is a man; but this dog, here, that's named John Carmichael is a dog, and he's named for the——"

"Nemmine," Herman interrupted, for Sam seemed to intend to continue his rather laborious explanation indefinitely. "Nemmine; I know whut you mean."

Penrod had become interested in Sam's idea, for the addition of two perfectly trained bloodhounds to the Jashber Agency would of course increase the agency's efficiency—at least dramatically. "Listen here, Sam," he said, "if Walter's got some bloodhound in him, I guess he could be trained that way, and Duke could help train him, because Duke's a full-blooded dog. Anyhow, we were thinkin' about lettin' you be a member after you came home, so I guess you can join. Look, Sam!"

With this simple prelude, he exposed the shield to Sam's surprised gaze, and forthwith explained the organization and purposes of the agency; Sam was given a special name and a number, thus becoming a full member, though of subordinate standing. The training of the bloodhounds then became the next order of business, and Duke was brought into the office to learn the first steps, in company with Walter-John.

"Our good ole bloodhounds got to have some practise," Penrod said. "That's the way we haf to begin, so they can learn what to do when we take 'em out after the Dade gang. This is the way we'll do——Listen, Sam! Listen, Herman! Listen, Verman! We'll make 'em smell sumpthing that belongs to one of us, then that one'll pretend like he's runnin' away and we'll let the good ole bloodhounds out after him. It wouldn't do for me to be the one, because of course Duke'd follow me anyway, and Sam won't do, because Walter'd follow him."

"It ain' go' be me," Herman announced quickly, as Penrod's eye wandered to him. "Ain' go' be no bloodhoun's pull me down an' hol' me fer no sheriffs!"

"Verman'd be the best one," Penrod said. "The

trouble is Verman hasn't got any shoes or hat or even any jacket." He paused in thought, then brightened. "That won't hurt, though. Just to begin with, we can make the good ole bloodhounds smell Verman, himself; then he can begin runnin' away, and we'll sick the good ole bloodhounds on him after he gets a start."

But Verman proved to be unwilling. "Mo!" he said decisively. "Mo!"

"Aw, look here, Verman!" Penrod said. "You don't want to go spoiling everything, do you? This isn't goin' to hurt you any, and you can't ack the cry-baby around here, or else I won't let you be Jim any longer. Come on now, we got to make these bloodhounds smell him good!"

"Mo!" Verman repeated, but with less determination; and, a moment later, as the noses of the two reluctant bloodhounds were forced against his person, he consented to take the part assigned to him in their training, and even giggled when his ribs were rubbed with the nose of Walter-John. "'Op picka me!" he protested.

Herman giggled, too, "Verman say stop ticklin' him," he interpreted.

"All right," Penrod said. "I guess these good ole

bloodhounds have smelled him enough, because they couldn't smell him any more if we kept at it a year, so run, Verman! Run!"

Verman ran out into the yard; the hounds were released and urged to follow the fugitive. "Sick 'im!" Penrod, Sam and Herman shouted. "Sick 'im, you ole bloodhounds you! Go after him! Sick 'im! Sick 'im!"

Thus encouraged, Duke and Walter-John behaved admirably. They ran after Verman, barked at him loudly, frisked round him with the liveliest pleasure in the world; Walter-John frolicsomely seized a loose edge of the largest patch upon Verman's trousers and held to it until a sound of ripping and Verman's aggrieved squealing abashed him into releasing it. Verman returned to the stable loudly complaining and holding the patch in place with his hand; but Sam was delighted and proud. "What did I tell you!" he shouted. "Didn't I tell you John Carmichael said John Carmichael was part bloodhound! C'm on, Verman, we'll make 'em smell you again, and this time I bet good ole John Carmichael'll——"

"Mo!" Verman said, and he remained obdurate, not to be persuaded. Herman declined positively to act as a substitute fugitive, and, as both Penrod and

Sam insisted that they were needed as trainers, it was finally decided to let the matter rest for the day upon the undoubted success of the single experiment.

"Anyway," Penrod said, "what we haf to do is to get some shoes or sumpthing that belong to the Dade gang and make our good ole bloodhounds smell 'em. Then they'd go after them the way they just did after Verman. F'r instance, if we had a pair of their shoes, we could have Verman wear 'em, and train Duke and Walter to go after Verman as long as he had the shoes on; then when the Dade gang put these shoes back on again—Whizz! Go it, you bloodhounds you!"

This idea struck him as so interesting that it recurred to him at intervals throughout the rest of the afternoon; and nothing could have been more natural than that it should recur to him again in the evening, when Mr. Dade, as matters fell out, left a light Panama hat upon the hall table. Margaret and the young man sat indoors, in the living-room, the air being chill, and Mr. Dade took his departure as usual at ten o'clock, a habit of his that had won Mrs. Schofield's favor and caused her to speak of him as a "well brought-up young man", which seemed, indeed, to be the fact. When he left, he did not put on his hat until after he had descended the verandah steps, Margaret having accompanied him so far; and then, employing it in a courtly gesture of farewell, "Good-night, Princess!" he said, and placed it upon his head. He experienced a slight surprise; but rather than spoil the effect of his departing gesture, he went out of the gate and a little way down the street before removing the hat and examining it by the light of a street-lamp. Yes, he was right; there were damp spots inside, upon the band and upon the fine straw, and there were also some smudges not there when he had deposited the hat upon the table. "Curious," he thought. Had water been spilled upon the table, or had someone else taken the hat temporarily by mistake?

However, the damage was insignificant, a fact more remarkable than he could have guessed, since Duke and Walter-John had spent whole minutes with their noses held firmly within the hat, and Verman had worn it during several practise excursions as a fugitive in the dusk of the alley. "Curious," Mr. Dade thought again, as he replaced the hat upon his head and resumed his way down the street. Then suddenly, he started nervously and quickened his pace.

A peculiar voice, with which, however, he was now

far from unfamiliar, had squealed out of the darkness almost at his heels. "Wam mubbowm!"

Then another voice at a distance seemed to repeat this squealing, though the words it cried came not distinguishably to the ears of Mr. Dade.

Penrod and Sam, farther in the rear, understood this second voice, however. It was that of Herman, interpreting for the small brother. "'Where 'em bloodhoun's?' Verman say, 'Where 'em bloodhoun's?'"

"Doggone it!" Penrod muttered. For Duke trotted amiably enough by his side, but only looked dejected, or stopped altogether, when urged forward upon the chase; and Sam, a little way behind, was even less successful with Walter-John. Walter-John, indeed, could be kept upon the trail only by means of a leash, and followed Sam in a partly sitting-down attitude, offering the dead weight of a complete, if passive, resistance.

"I expeck he wants to go home," Sam panted, when he and his charge came up with Penrod. "Anyhow he seems to want to sit down all the time. I guess bloodhounds don't like to work at night, Penrod, proba'ly. John Carmichael don't seem to take any interest, like he did this afternoon, and besides, I got to go home, myself, because I'm goin' to get fits for stayin' out this late, anyhow."

They paused for consultation; but stood for a time in silence, and then, from the farther end of the next block, heard faintly another appeal from Verman, and, a moment later, almost as faintly, the faithful brother's interpretation, "Verman say he cain' see no bloodhoun's!"

"Well, what we better do?" Sam inquired, looking down moodily at the bloodhounds. Duke had taken occasion to roll upon his back, and Walter-John was sniffing at him indolently. "We better call to Herman and Verman we're goin' home now, don't you think, Penrod?"

"I don't s'pose we could make 'em hear us," Penrod said. "Not unless we ran after 'em, and I got to go home now, too, Sam. It's better to let them go on shadowin' him, anyway." Then, as the two boys turned, and, followed by the bloodhounds, walked back toward home, he went on: "I guess you're right about our good ole dogs not likin' to go after crooks except in daytime, Sam. We got to teach 'em to trail the Dade gang while it's light, I guess, and I know what'd be the best time for that. Sunday afternoon before last he and my sister went for a walk, and

hey went last Sunday, too. If they go again next
Sunday, why, we can get Herman and Verman and
our good ole bloodhounds——"

"Listen!" Sam said.

In the quiet night a far away shrilling in a slender
African voice was just audible; then the sound seemed
to be repeated like an echo a little louder than the
original outcry.

"Could you make out anything he said?" Sam
asked.

"No; they're too far down the street. They're
mighty good men, that ole Jim and Bill. They'll
keep right on the trail until he goes home to bed. It's
a good thing for us that Jim and Bill are colored, I
expeck."

Sam was surprised. "Why?" he inquired.

"Well, for one thing, you can't see 'em very well
after dark," Penrod answered. "And besides," the
observant boy added, a moment later, "colored
people never haf to go home to bed at night, anyhow."

XVI

A SUNDAY STROLL

THE following Sunday morning, Mr. Robert Williams went to church in company with the other members of his own family—that is to say, with his father and his mother and his eleven-year-old brother, Sam. The serious expression of the new Bachelor of Arts was one evidence that going to church with his own family was not one of the summer pleasures he had promised himself in his undergraduate day-dreams, and, during the service, his eyes frequently wandered to another family group of four in a pew across the aisle. On the homeward way, also, his wistful look ran forward, over intervening heads, to where, in this other family group, a frivolous hat affected sedateness for the occasion. No physical force prevented Robert from joining Miss Schofield; she had no escort or protection except that afforded by her father, mother and brother. Nevertheless, Robert Williams walked with his own family—in peace, it may be, but certainly without jocosity.

In the afternoon, after four o'clock, he came out upon the front verandah of his father's house, sat in a wicker chair and opened a book, but read nothing therein. His gaze was steadfast upon a lawn and gate a little way down the street, and there was in his face an expectancy like that of a person who waits in a dentist's anteroom. It was the look of one who, from previous experience, knows what is going to happen presently but anticipates little to his pleasure.

Nor did his inward prophecies fail of fulfilment—though, as it happened, the facts proved to be an unexpected and fantastic embroidery upon the simple weave of his predictions. From Mr. Schofield's gate,

as the disturbed Robert expected, Margaret and Mr
Herbert Hamilton Dade came forth, patently for an
afternoon walk; and both were in a mood of gaiety
so far as sight and hearing might disclose their con
dition to the young man pretending to read a book
The cruel Margaret had looked never more charming

She and her handsome companion passed along the
Williams's fence, and Robert caught the word "Princess" in Mr. Dade's melodious voice, but bent in-
terestedly over his book and did not look up until
they had gone by. When he did lift his eyes, it seemed
to him that he caught just the end of a swift gesture
of Margaret's head; he had the impression that she
had glanced back over her shoulder at him.

"Coquette!" he breathed; and then he viciously
muttered the word, "Princess!" So she liked *that*
awful sort of thing! And Robert remembered a class-
mate of his who had printed a poem, evidently
personal and particular, called "Milady", in a college
paper early in the first freshman term, and thus ac-
quired a nickname that had to be carefully explained
to the poet's father on class-day, four years later.
"Princess!" said Robert. "Oh, *all* right!"

He watched this girl of execrable taste as she sauntered up the sunshiny pavement beside Mr. Dade,

nd, though he loathed her romantic tendencies, he
could not help feeling that her dress was the prettiest
he had ever seen her wear—incomparably prettier
than any dress he had ever seen any other girl wear.
And she was so graceful! In the light breeze her
chiffon overskirt fluttered like sunbeams on a rapid
brook. He could have seen it better, he noted with
annoyance, if that little darkey boy had not walked
so close behind her. The little darkey boy seemed
to be intending to pass Margaret and Mr. Dade and
walk ahead of them, the gloomy watcher observed,
but just at the last moment, when he was close along-
side, he always changed his mind and fell back. About
ten paces behind him walked another colored boy,
a larger one.

Suddenly, Robert's book fell to the floor of the
verandah. Thirty or forty feet behind the second
colored boy walked Sam Williams, Robert's brother,
leading the large, reluctant pup, John Carmichael,
upon a leash, and, at about the same distance to the
rear of Sam came one wearing an imperious—nay,
almost satanic—intensity of countenance, evidently
in command. This person was he whom Robert may
most creditably be represented as defining, mentally,
as "that blank Penrod". Penrod was accompanied

by Duke, and at times seemed to address him vehemently, though in undertones. The observer's eyes
became luminous with wonder and curiosity. Unmistakably, here was some sort of procession!

Robert had no impulse to interfere. If those two
small negroes and Sam and Penrod and John Carmichael and Duke found themselves interested in
taking a walk, as it were, with Miss Schofield and her
dashing admirer, what right had any outsider to
intervene? And particularly on the part of a dis-
qualified suitor must any attempt to break up the
little parade have appeared an intrusion. However, as
it passed up the street, he felt warranted in going as
far as the gate to look at it.

Mr. Dade and Margaret had reached the next
corner; but Robert was able to see that Mr. Dade
began to be annoyed by the persistent proximity of
the smaller negro. In fact, over his shoulder, Mr.
Dade seemed to be addressing the little negro harshly,
and the latter, to all appearances, was making a
voluble and gesticulative but unsatisfactory reply.
The other colored boy, standing aloof, was calling
something in the direction of Sam and Penrod, who
had each moved aside from the line of vision of Mr.
Dade and Margaret—Sam behind a shade-tree, and

enrod behind an ornamental stone upon an open lawn,
here he had prostrated himself. The whole proceed-
ng was somewhat conspicuous, and several people
cross the street had paused to observe it. However,
Ir. Dade presently abandoned his argument, and
e and Margaret turned the corner, as closely at-
ended by the small negro boy as before. The larger
ne followed; Penrod rose cautiously; Sam came
rom behind his tree, and, a moment later, both
f them, and their placidly accompanying dogs, dis-
ppeared in the same direction.

Robert was profoundly interested; but his dignity
lid not permit him to add one more to the procession.
A grimness that was far cousin to a smile came to his
ips, and, as he retired into the house, the least little
ightening of his sorrows was perceptible upon his
ountenance. As the afternoon waned and no
ound or sign of a returning Sam indicated that the
uninvited strollers had grown disheartened in their
mysterious purpose, this alleviation of Robert's
ncreased, so that he appeared at the evening table
vith a livelier air than his worried mother had seen
upon him since the day of his return from college.
Ie even helped Sam in the latter's excuses for being
a full ten minutes late, and, after the meal was over,

sought that youth's company in the twilight of th
back yard. He began by giving Sam a quarter
Sam was sincerely grateful, though hurried.

"I'm cert'nly much obliged," he said, movin;
toward the back fence. "Well, I guess I got to b·
goin'."

"Where do you have to go, Sam?"

"Over to Penrod's."

"What for?"

"Oh, nothin'."

"Going to play with Penrod and those two colorec
boys?"

"I dunno," said Sam; and, noting a tendency o·
the part of Robert to detain him with more conver
sation, he added: "Well, I'm very much obliged
Bob. Well, g'-by!" And he set his hand upon th·
fence to climb it.

"Wait a minute, can't you? I just wanted to——'

"Honest, I got to go!"

And in confirmation, there came a shout from th·
alley. It was the voice of Herman. "Hi, Tabber!" i·
shouted.

"I'm comin', Bill," Sam called in response.

"We goin' begin, Tabber," Herman shoutec
again. "Ole Jawge, he waitin' on you."

"I'm comin', ain't I?"

But as Sam reached the top of the fence, a detaining hand was laid upon his shoulder. "I only want to talk to you a minute, Sam."

"Honest, Bob, I *got* to go. I got——"

Robert gave Sam another quarter.

"Well, much obliged," said Sam, descending from the fence. "What you want to talk about?"

"Who was it that called you just then?"

"It's Herman; he's a colored boy."

"What name did he call you?"

"Oh, nothin'. 'Tabber', I guess. We kind of pretend we got other names. Penrod said I'd be Tabber." Sam laughed a little sheepishly. "He made it up, I guess."

"Who's George?"

"It's Penrod." Here Sam laughed again. "He's George—George B. Jashber. Herman's Bill and Verman's Jim and I'm Tabber. They only took me in a few days ago, when I went over there."

"What were you all doing this afternoon, Sam?"

"When?"

"Following Penrod's sister and—and her friend all over town."

Sam at once looked serious. "Well, that part of it

isn't playin' at all. It's—it's a perty danger's biznuss."

"So! How is it dangerous?"

Before Sam could reply, the cry came again from the alley. "Hi, Tabber! You *comin'*?"

"Can't you wait a *minute*?" Sam responded impatiently. "Honest, Bob, I *can't* stay any——"

"Oh, yes, you can," said Robert. "For fifty cents."

"Well, where's——"

"I mean the fifty cents I've already given you," Robert explained.

"Oh," Sam said rather blankly, and then, appreciating the justice of his brother's argument, he inquired, "What you want me to do?"

"Tell me what is the dangerous business, and why you and the other boys were following those two this afternoon. First, how long did you follow them?"

"Till they came back," Sam said, with admirable simplicity.

"Well, I always did believe in young people being carefully chaperoned," said Robert thoughtfully. "It seems to me you boys behaved quite properly in this matter, Sam. What did *they* do?"

"You goin' to tell papa and mamma?"

"I won't tell anybody at all."

"Well, they got kind of mad, I guess," Sam admitted. "First, they wanted Verman to keep away from 'em, but they couldn't understand anything he said, and I guess they thought he was just goin' the way they were, anyhow; so they went on, way out perty near to the new park, and when they got out there, they stood around on the new bridge a good while, and then this ole Dade he tried to chase Verman back, but he couldn't catch him. Well, and then he and Margaret went and sat around on a bench. So, afterwhile, they got up and started home, and ole Dade he just *wouldn't* let Verman keep anywheres near 'em. He kep' chasin' him back all the time, and once he chased him perty near a square— but every time 'course Verman'd come back again, and then he'd chase him again, and Herman, too. He never saw me and Penrod but sometimes lots of other people did, and they'd kind o' laugh or sumpthing, and ole Dade, 'course he thought it was all Verman's fault—but he never did catch him."

"Thank you, Sam," said Robert, and, to Sam's surprise, his brother's voice was so affable that it was almost tender. "Now, if you'll just tell me what it's all about, I won't keep you any longer. What did you boys do it *for?* What were you up to?"

Sam looked embarrassed, and laughed. "Well—

we kind of thought we could train John Carmichael and Duke to be bloodhounds; but I guess we got to give it up. They're awful stubborn about not learning what we want 'em to."

"I see," Robert said. "But what I want to know, Sam, is why you were following Margaret and Mr. Dade."

Sam stepped closer and spoke in a low tone. "Well, Penrod's a detective, now," he said confidentially.

"You mean you boys play he's one."

"No," Sam insisted earnestly. "He *is !* He's a real one. Honest he is, Bob! He's got a badge and everything. He's Number Hunderd and Three. It's the honest truth, and I wouldn't believe him, myself, if he hadn't showed me the badge. He had to pay a whole lot of money for it, honest! He's got a right to shadow anybody he wants to, and he's got a right to tell anybody else to go and shadow 'em, and they got a right to do it. It's the law."

"All right," said Robert. "But what were you doing this afternoon?"

"We were just out shadowin'. We go out shadowin' that ole Dade all the time. Some days we don't all keep after him, because Herman and Verman got to do a lot o' work around their house; but most o' the time they come along, and they keep right up close to him because Verman's tongue-tied."

"I don't see what that's got to do with it."

"Well, listen, Bob," said Sam, obviously believing his explanation ample. "Listen! Herman can understand everything he says; but this ole Dade can't understand a word. Ole Dade tried to kick him four or five times lately; but I don't believe there's anybody in the world can kick Verman. He knows how to get out o' the way when anybody kicks at him better'n any boy I ever knew in my life."

"How does it happen you all like to go out shadowing Mr. Dade, Sam? How'd you decide on him?"

"Why, I told you," said Sam. "Penrod's a detective. He found it all out."

"Found what out?"

"About ole Dade bein' a crook."

"What are you talking about, Sam?"

"Why, he *is* a crook!" Sam exclaimed. "Isn't he, Bob? Don't you think so?"

"Well——" Robert hesitated. "I understood that he was going to organize a new insurance company with Mr. Paoli Jones and his brother Montgomery. I didn't know that was criminal, precisely. What does Penrod say he found out?"

"Penrod says first he found out ole Dade steals horses."

"No! Did he?"

"Don't you believe it?"

"Well, I don't know," said Robert musingly. "Penrod is a very intelligent boy, it seems to me. I *hope* he hasn't made a mistake about this."

"Well, that isn't the worst," Sam continued, becoming eager under the encouragement of his brother's benevolent manner. "He does *lots* worse'n that!"

"What, Sam?"

"Well, you just said yourself he was doin' *sumpthing* to Marjorie Jones's father and her uncle."

"Well——"

"Well, Penrod found out this ole Dade is goin' to get Marjorie Jones's uncle drunk, and then he's goin' to kill him or sumpthing, and make Marjorie Jones's father sign some ole papers, and take his house an' lot away from him or sumpthing, and get married to Margaret. Penrod says we got to shadow him every minute, because ole Dade's liable to take and do it any day. He's over there now, and that's what I got to go for. We got to keep shadowin' him until we haf to go to bed."

"Run along," said Robert. "I'll ask mother to let

you stay out an extra half-hour before she calls you. But here——" He fumbled in his pocket. "Here's another quarter. It's not for you; it's for Penrod. Tell him it's a secret, though; he mustn't mention that I sent it to him. Penrod's a nice boy, Sam. I'm glad you're such a friend of his."

And as Sam dropped to the other side of the fence, Mr. Robert Williams decided that he liked boys. Wholesome, fine, sensible creatures, he thought them; and, with his hands in his empty pockets, he strolled round the block under the starlight, whistling. But his whistling stopped momentarily as he passed along the Schofields' fence and his ear caught strange, animal-like sounds—not very like. An owl was evidently meant to hoot, and there was a protracted chorus of barking that never would have interested Penrod Schofield's little old dog, Duke.

Robert went on, his renewed whistling loud and cheery.

XVII

THE PURSUIT CONTINUES

THE next morning Robert received a letter, written and posted late the previous evening. The girlish handwriting, pretty and appealing, showed signs of jerkiness here and there, seeming to reveal that the writer had been subject to agitation as she wrote. Robert paid a more flattering attention to this phenomenon than to the direct and intentional substance of the missive.

ROBERT:

I really was *so* amused at your pretending to read a book and not even speaking to old friends as they pass your

ouse. I should think if college had done you much good,
ou would still be polite enough to at least bow to old
riends. I suppose you are still cross over what I said that
vening. I don't care, because it was just for your own
ood and didn't have anything to do with what you were
onsensical enough to accuse me of, anyhow. I should
eally like to know what on earth is the matter with you.
ust because a girl shows a passing interest in somebody
lse she may hardly know at all except in the most super-
icial way, and might even find tiresome or ridiculous if she
aw too much of such a person, I think nothing could be
illier than her old friends behaving with *actual rudeness*
o her for such an absurd reason. I have always been taught
hat good manners were just as necessary between old
riends as they were anywhere—but, of course, I may be
vrong.

> Sincerely,
> MARGARET PASSLOE SCHOFIELD.

That afternoon, being again in funds, Robert gave
Sam a dollar. Sam's amazement fully equaled his
gratitude.

"Well, I cert'nly am much obliged!" he gasped.

"I want you to give half of it to Penrod," Robert
said affably. "He's a boy the more I think about him
the more I *like* to think about him. Ah——" He paused.
"There's something more I'd like to ask you about
what happened yesterday afternoon, Sam."

"You mean about our havin' to give up training
the bloodhounds?"

"No," Robert said. "No, I wasn't thinking of that—not particularly, Sam. Of course it does seem too bad that you've had to give the bloodhounds up because they certainly did add to the effect, as it were! But what I wanted to ask was whether or not quite a number of people happened to notice the proceedings yesterday afternoon. You told me that some people did notice, and I think you mentioned that they laughed. Is that correct?"

"Yes," Sam informed him casually. "I expect mostly they were laughin' at Verman as we were goin' along. Sometimes people out on their porches kind of laughed, and a few times people clear on the other side of the street laughed and sort of pointed."

"I see. Did you happen to notice Margaret Schofield, Sam? Ah—did she seem to mind it at all?"

"Well, I kind of expeck so. She was red all the time and walked pretty fast. When ole Dade got so excited and went to chasin' Verman and tryin' to kick him and everything, she was awful red, because that was out at the park where the most people were, and a lot of 'em were laughin' pretty loud, and some of 'em kind of yelled when Verman would dodge. Yes, I guess she was pretty mad, because she stayed

d and walked home terrible fast. I expeck it was a
ood thing for Penrod she never saw him and didn't
now he had anything to do with it."

"Yes, I suppose so," Robert assented. "But Pen-
od's a fine outstanding boy, Sam, and you mustn't
orget to give him half of that dollar."

"No, I won't; I'll give it to him right away."

"I suppose you're going on with your game—not
game', I mean to say——"

"You mean about ole Dade?"

"Yes," said Robert, "that dangerous business you
vere speaking of last night. Are you boys going on
vith it to-day?"

"Why, 'course!"

"Don't let me keep you, then," said Robert
politely. "Not for a minute!"

Nevertheless, he called Sam back, after the latter
had started, and gave him a dime for Herman and
one for Verman.

When Sam, bringing these financial encourage-
ments, reached the agency in Penrod's stable, George
B. Jashber and Bill and Jim, that is to say, Nos. 103,
104 and 105 (or George B. and his men) felt that
they were making real progress. Elated, they went

at once to the corner drug store, where each had an afternoon pick-me-up of soda-water thickened by ice-cream and sweet flavoring sirup. Then, carrying with them salted peanuts, salted almonds, cinnamon drops, sticks of liquorice, a bag of large, soggy balls of cocoanut-sugar and flour, and a terrible thing almost a foot long, purchased at the grocery and known to them as a "b'loney sausage", they returned to the stable and performed the rite of the Daily Report. The notes taken by George B. on this occasion were sketchier than usual, since the utterance of Bill and Tabber, impeded by mastication, was not much more intelligible than that of Jim. However, since these notes covered the shadowing of the previous day in which all members of the organization had taken part, their fragmentary nature was probably of no great detrimental importance.

Nor were the chief and his subordinates at all disturbed by the fact that this report showed nothing more discreditable to Mr. Dade than that he had taken a walk with Penrod's sister and had displayed irritation with Verman and, subsequently, with Herman. Indeed, there was no reason why the members of the agency should have been more discouraged by this report than by any other in Penrod's collec-

ion, for all the others were as innocuous. The trail
f the scondrel, Dade, led sometimes from the
Y. M. C. A. building to Jones Brothers' real-estate
ffice, sometimes to a barber shop, sometimes to a
dairy-lunch or other restaurant, sometimes to the
post-office—and always, when the shadowers persisted
ong enough, back to the Y. M. C. A. building. There
were times when the scondrel had been tracked to
a confectioner's, and twice he had gone to a florist's;
but not once did a report prove him to have entered a
saloon. The truth is that a grown person, examining
these documents, must have judged Mr. Dade to be
certainly harmless and probably exemplary; and, if
the young man had known of their existence, he
might well have cited them in a court of law (suppos-
ing such necessity) as proof of his good habits and
testimony to his high character. But whoever sur-
mises that the reports lacked damnatory significance
in the eyes of the agency understands little of George
B. Jashber, Bill, Jim and honest Tabber. They had
begun by accepting it as a fact that this ole Dade was
guilty; therefore, whatever he did was suspicious.
The nature of his guilt remained indefinite; sometimes it was one thing, sometimes another. On certain
days, he would be spoken and thought of as a man

who stole horses; on other days, his habitual crim
seemed to be obtaining possession of some ole father'
house an' lot through the signing of some ole papers
But never for one moment was there any doubt tha
he was a criminal. In that capacity, he was securel
established—it might be said, indeed, that he ha
been appointed to the office; he was the official croo
of this agency. One noontime, Penrod and Sam shad
owed him to a business-men's revival meeting; the
even followed him inside, and nothing that he di
there shook their constant faith that in selecting hin
to be the agency's crook Penrod had done well.

And in this—as in other ways of boys, whose
ways, fundamentally, are grown people's ways, anc
of whom nearly all human truth may be learned—
in this we see a plain old fact of life prettily confirmed
that once we judge, we no longer possess judgment
That is the reason why grown people who have de
cided to think of certain other people as enemies, or
as bad people, are shocked and troubled (for the
moment) when they hear of those enemies or bad
people doing something worthy and creditable. The
worthy and creditable action is interpreted, in such
cases, as the deceptive result of vicious motives.
George B. Jashber, Bill, Jim and Tabber merely

mitted the pause for being shocked and doing the
interpreting. Thus, the report of ole Dade's visit to
the revival meeting was written simply:

Report. Nomber 103 George B. Jashber and Nomber
96 Tabber shad to where lots going on like praying and
l such The crook got to senging hims.

XVIII

TWO RETURN TO PRIVATE LIFE

THE condition of Mr. Herbert Hamilto
Dade's nerves may be described—thoug
imperfectly—as shaken. What had fir
seemed to him merely annoying coincidence ha
been so persistently repeated that it was folly t
think the phenomena could be accounted for by eve
the most fantastic stretching of the laws of chanc
Ordinarily he was not a superstitious young mar
nevertheless, his mind had begun to be haunted b
uncomfortable, strange ideas; he knew that the day

of bewitchment were long since passed; but he had become so sensitive that he was ready to start at the mere sight of colored children on the street—and that in broad daylight. Then, in the Y. M. C. A. library, early on an evening of rain, he found a book on Voodooism that did little to reassure him; he could not read it without glancing apprehensively over his shoulder from time to time, and after an hour he decided that this work, though learned, was making him morbid. He closed the book abruptly, returned it to its shelf, then went downstairs to the vestibule of the building. Here he paused for some moments of perturbed thought, and his expression was that of a person who debates whether or not to make an experiment that his forebodings warn him will end ominously. Then, with a hand slightly tremulous, he pushed open the outer door. It yielded with reluctance to his touch, as if resisted by something not weighty but unwilling to be dislodged from the step.

"He hum ow!" shouted a querulous voice too well known to him. "He hoohum me how in haim!"

Herman, at the corner of the building, interpreted to Penrod, lurking beyond. "He say ole Dade comin' out. Say he pushin' him out in the rain. I reckon

Verman gittin' kine o' mad. We gittin' might tired all 'iss shaddin' an' ev'ything. When we go' git a chance to quit an' do somp'm' else?"

"Well, what's the matter of you?" Penrod demanded crossly, approaching him. "My goodness! I'd like to know what you and Verman *want!*"

"Want to go home an' quit all 'iss shaddin'. Look to me like I nev' git so wet in my days."

"You want to *quit?*" Penrod asked incredulously.

"I sut ny do!" Herman responded with fervor. "'Isshere fofe time I be'n wet froo clean to my skin, an' I don' keer what ole Dade do no mo'. I ain' see no hosses, an' I ain' see no ole papuhs he done sign, an' I ain' liable to see none, 'cause he don' nev' sign none when we 'roun the place. How we go' ketch 'im at it? Look to me like he mus' always sign 'em inside 'isshere buildin', else sometime when we home eatin' meals 'r else in bed. Anyways, I don' keer what he do no mo'. We be'n goin' on 'iss way an' shaddin', shaddin' all time, shaddin' I dunno how long, an' I'm a-goin' quit!"

"You ain't goin' to quit *now*, are you, Bill?" his chief asked reproachfully.

"Aft' 'iss one night, you kin fill my place," said Herman firmly. "I done got so tired all 'isshere

shaddin', shaddin', all time shaddin', I ain' bettin'
no man I ain' go' drop dead in my tracks."

This was not the first time Penrod had dealt with
mutiny of the sort; in fact, if he had not been chief,
holding the delightful power to send his men here
or there as he chose, and to say, "Do thus", or "Do
so", at will, he would have tired long since, himself. But, as things were, he was both grieved and
irritated by Herman's complaints.

"My goodness!" he remonstrated. "Haven't you
got any *sense*, Herman? I guess you don't remember
there's mighty few colored boys get a *chance* like
this."

"Chanst like whut? You gimme chanst fer to walk
my feet off, git wet froo to my skin, 'n'en git the hide
lammed off o' me when I git back home! 'At's all
chanst you gimme!"

"My goodness! I never did hear anybody that
liked to talk so much! Now, you kept standin'
around here so long talkin', ole Dade's come out——"

"No, he ain'."

"Well, Verman hollered and said——"

"I don' keer what he hollered. He's settin' back
scrooged up ag'in' the do', out the rain, like whut
he wuz. Ole Dade come out, gone back in ag'in.'"

This was accurate, except that Mr. Dade had not come out. At the sound of Verman's voice, he instantly allowed the door to close and withdrew to the interior of the building. His manner was pre-occupied, not without perturbation. He declined a game of checkers with a fellow lodger, and, after a few moments of indecision in the reading-room, went upstairs to his own chamber, where he sat upon the edge of his bed and looked long and thoughtfully at his trunk.

The rain beat furiously upon the window of his room; necessarily it was copious upon Penrod and the despondent Herman, some forty feet beneath that window. Verman was lucky enough to obtain a measure of shelter; but suffered a misfortune, which caused him so greatly to distrust the doorway that he abandoned it definitely. A basket-ball team of hearty young men, all in high spirits and well equipped against the weather, came bursting forth from the building with such sudden gusto and liveli-ness that Verman, pressed too tightly against the door, found an almost infinitesimal portion of his person, together with a fold of his trousers, caught between the base of the door and the sill and acting as a wedge to prevent the door from opening readily; but, as the full force of the basket-ball team accumulated against this momentary resistance, the door flew open, and Verman, uttering a dolorous shout, sped before it. Seated, he passed to the middle of the splashing sidewalk, and in other postures proceeded as far as the street. Then, having risen, he did not pause, but started at once for home. He went hastily, yet in the attitude of one who nurses himself in affliction, and, upon being joined by Penrod and Herman, kept hurrying on his way, in spite of Penrod's every remonstrance. His attire was damaged, and he had been seriously pinched. With bitterness, he declined to return to his post —and resigned. Herman also resigned.

The next morning, not appearing at the agency, and being summoned (from the alley doors of the carriage-house) for the Report, the brothers came into the stable and resigned again.

"Well, listen, if you ever heard anybody talk like they hadn't got a grain o' sense!" Penrod exclaimed to Sam. Sam, having been detained at home the night before, was still loyal. "Looky here, Herman," the chief went on, turning to the former members, "I guess you got better sense than you act like. What you and Verman want to go and quit

now for? Look: Not hardly two weeks ago—didn't
you each get a dime, besides all that food Sam and
I bought and let you eat as much of as we ate, ourselves?"

"Dime!" said Herman coldly. "We ain' got no
mo' dime now. Yes; an' whut come when we gone et
all 'at b'loney sausage an' sody an' ev'y which an'
whut? Done h'ist me so bad I ain' sca'cely et nuff'm
sense but whut she like to h'ist me ag'in! Me an'
Verman froo, I tell you!"

Penrod turned appealingly to Verman. "Well, if
ole Herman *has* got to act like he hasn't got a grain
o' sense, I bet good ole Verman isn't goin' back on
Sam and me. Verman, *you* know what's good for
you, don't you, Verman? Verman, *you're* goin' to
keep on——"

"Mo!" Verman exclaimed immediately. "*Mo!*"

"Verman, he set on quittin' wuss'n I am," said
Herman. "Mammy couldn' sca'cely fix him his
pants so's he kin walk roun' nowhere; an' he got sech
a pinch' place on him, she say she almos' goin' feel
sorry to lam' him fer nex' week er two. I don' keer ef
ole Mis' Dade steal how many hosses, an' I don'
keer ef he tuck an' run away wif fo' millyum house
an' lots! I done walk my feet off shaddin', shaddin',

all time shaddin', an' I done got soak' froo to my skin an' bones, an' nev' *see* nuff'm' 'mount to nuff'm' nohow. I done walk my feet off fer las' time, I tell you! *No*, suh; me an' Verman *quit!*"

It seemed to be final.

XIX

DISASTER

AFTER lunch, Sam and Penrod sat dispiritedly
in the office, lacking heart to take up the
chase or even to proceed with the day's
Report. Before long, they drifted out into the yard,
and thence to the sidewalk, saying little, for they
began to feel that the great days of the agency
were over, and gloomily they were wondering what
they could find to take its place. The conduct of
Herman and Verman appeared in a light purely hate-

252

ful. Just when everything was going so well—and everything——

"Penrod! Penrod Schofield!"

From down the street came the lovely voice of Marjorie Jones, calling. She was running toward them, waving her arms eagerly and crying Penrod's name in excitement. The boys listlessly watched her approach.

"Penrod!" she gasped, as she reached them. She leaned against the fence, trying to recover her breath. "Oh, Penrod! Oh, my!"

"Well, what's the matter of you, Marjorie?"

"Papa!" she panted. "Pup-papa—papa wants you to come to our house. He wants to see you before he goes back down town to his office."

"What for?" Penrod asked, surprised.

"About—oh, my, I did run so fast! About—it's about that ole crook, Penrod!"

Penrod stared, incredulous. He felt suddenly uncomfortable, and a vague apprehension stirred within him.

"He wants you to come right away. It's all on account of because I told him all that stuff you told me. I told papa all that stuff you told me——"

"What—what stuff?"

"About ole Dade, Penrod. I told papa every bit you said, and what you think: papa says you haf to come and *tell* him about it!"

"What you talkin' about, Marjorie? What you— what you talkin' so much about?"

"Why, about what you told me about that ole crook," Marjorie informed him cheerfully. "I told papa all about that shadowin' and everything—and I told him how you found out this ole Dade was such a crook, and how you said he was goin' to get papa to sign some ole papers and get his house an' lot, and maybe he'd kill Uncle Montgomery or maybe not—because you know you weren't sure about that part, Penrod—and, well, I told papa everything about it."

"When?" Penrod asked, and a sudden chill played along his spine. "When did you tell him about it?"

"Just a little while ago, while we were having lunch. Papa was saying to mamma he thought Mr. Dade was such a nice young man, and so they noticed I was makin' a face and asked me what for. Well, mamma always scolds me for makin' faces, so you see I had to tell why I did it, and then was when I told papa all about everything you said about ole Dade. When I told him you said your

own father and mother told you he stole horses,
papa said they must of been joking or sumpthing,
and he would ask your father about that, this evening, maybe; but first he told me to come and bring
you over to our house right away, so you could tell
him where you had heard all those other things about
ole Dade's getting him to sign papers and everything.
So hurry and come on, Penrod, 'cause he's waiting.
You can come, too, Sam, if you want to."

"Me?" Sam looked at Penrod, who stood staring
open-mouthed at Marjorie. "No," Sam said uneasily. "I guess I got to be gettin' along home
perty soon. I expeck I ought to go give John Carmichael a bath or sumpthing, proba'ly."

"Come on, Penrod," Marjorie urged. "Papa said
he wanted you to come right away."

But an increasing perturbation had seized upon
Penrod. "Right away?" he said, frowning. "I don't
believe I ought to—anyhow not right away, Marjorie."

"What!" she cried indignantly. "When my papa
says——"

"Well, I guess I got to ast my mother first," Penrod interrupted, with a heat of conscience never before perceived in him by either of his present com-

panions. "I can't go unless my mother *says* I can, I guess, can I?"

"Well, run ast her," said Marjorie, somewhat taken aback but retaining her presence of mind. "I'll wait for you while you run and——"

"She might not be home," Penrod objected. "She might of gone out somewhere. I shouldn't be supprised if she went out to see an' ole aunt o' mine that lives 'way out in the country. I guess that must be where she did go."

"She did not!" Marjorie asserted. "I saw her lookin' out of a window at us about two minutes ago. Hurry, Penrod! Run ask her, and I'll wait. Of course she'll let you if you tell her *papa* wants you."

Penrod seemed to deliberate. "Well, locky here," he said slowly. "This is the best way we better fix it. You go on ahead, because I expeck you better hurry; and I'll go on upstairs and ast Mamma if I can go over to your house, and then if she says I can——"

"Why, of *course* she will!"

"Well, if she does, I'll hurry and run after you and proba'ly catch you before you get there. You better start right away, Marjorie."

She looked perplexed and a little troubled. "Well, why don't you go ast your mother—if you're going to, Penrod?"

"Well, I am." He walked toward the front door. "I'm goin' in just as soon as you start."

"Well——" Marjorie said irresolutely; but his suggestion seemed plausible—or perhaps she felt herself ill-equipped for further argument with him. At all events, she began to move toward home, at the same time looking back over her shoulder and making gestures to urge greater haste upon him. "Please, hurry!" she called. "I'll tell papa you're comin' right away." Then she trotted off down the street obediently, with the sunshine dancing prettily through her undulating amber curls.

But Penrod, gazing after her, as he continued to move at a snail's pace toward the house, found little pleasure in this picture, and the expression of uneasiness upon the countenance of Master Williams had deepened, though, naturally, this uneasiness of Sam's was far less than that of his friend. For the moment, both boys were inarticulate; yet undoubtedly they shared in a common emotion, to which Sam finally gave a certain amount of expression. "Well, anyhow," he said plaintively, "I and Herman and Verman never did a single thing you didn't tell us to, Penrod."

The implications of this bit of self-defense were voluminous, so to speak, and fell upon Penrod heavily. Already, he began to look horrified; it might have been thought that he was not in the best of health. For the thing that a boy most shrinks from—that is, having his private affairs exposed, and himself involved in the mysteries of grown-up jurisprudence, where intentions go for nothing and all is incalculable and ominous—this thing, it seemed, was happening to him.

"Well——" he said, and, swallowing heavily, said nothing more.

"She's motioning to you to go on in and ask your mother," Sam said, still gazing down the street after Marjorie, and he added, with severity, "You better hurry and do it, too, because I guess the sooner you get there the better for you, Penrod!" He turned toward his own home, and, although his uneasiness remained upon him, he contrived to assume the air of a self-righteous person not involved in consequences probably about to descend upon people of questionable conduct. "I can't hang around here any longer,"

ne said, as if in reply to a suggestion that caused him
some indignation. "I guess John Carmichael's got a
right to have a bath once this summer, anyway!
Even a poor dog's got a right to expeck a little good
treatment and not to haf to let his fleas eat him up
alive!"

Virtuously, Sam quickened his pace to go upon this
honorable errand, his attitude, as he went, eloquently
expressing the conviction that whoever else might be
in grave trouble he wasn't in any whatever, himself,
and ought not to be.

Penrod went into the house.

A few minutes later, his mother stood at the foot
of the attic stairway. "Penrod!" she called.
"Penrod!"

There was silence. She mounted to the top of the
stairway and looked about her. "Penrod!" she called
again; then, listening intently, followed a very faint
noise—the noise made by a button gently rubbing
upon a board—and found her son unostentatiously
crawling along the floor between some trunks and the
wall. "Good gracious!" she cried. "I almost thought
there was a burglar up here. What on earth are you
doing?"

"I lost sumpthing," he said thickly.

"What was it?"

"Ma'am?"

"What are you looking for?"

"Well—it's a top."

"You couldn't have lost it up here. How absurd
If that isn't just like a boy—to come looking for a los*
top in the attic! Get up, Penrod!"

"Ma'am?"

"Get up! You can't play up here; the heat's
enough to give you a sunstroke. Get up at once
and——" But as he obeyed her, rising to his feet, she
uttered a cry of dismay. "Penrod! You're nothing but
dust and cobwebs! It'll be a mercy if your clothes
aren't ruined! Go down to the bathroom this minute
and wash your face and hands in hot water. Then get
a whisk-broom and a clothes-brush and come to me,
and I'll see what can be done! Run!"

Penrod ran; at least, he made haste. At the bottom of the stairs, he turned in the direction of a bathroom but paused not at its door. Instead, he went
down the back stairs, out through the kitchen to the
back yard, thence to the woodshed. Hurriedly he
climbed the side of the tall sawdust box and disappeared from the sight of man and the light of day.

Two minutes later, he climbed out again, holding

something concealed in his hand. Cautiously peering from the woodshed doorway, he reconnoitered the horizon, then ran to the cistern, near the back porch, removed the iron cover, and dropped within the orifice that small object he had held clenched in his fingers. There was a faint splash, and, sliding down beneath the surface of the brown water, a silvery streak descended—and vanished. It was the shield of Pvt. Detec. No. 103, belonging to Gray Bros. Ag'cy, and thus it disappeared forever—or at least until that cistern should be renovated.

Then the former George B. Jashber, now no more than a small boy pale beneath cobwebs and coatings of dust—Penrod Schofield, in fact—scurried back to the woodshed and again hastily concealed himself in the sawdust box.

Calamity was upon him. On the instant when Marjorie spoke the words, "I told papa every bit you said", prophetic fear had seized him. And as she so blithely went on with her artless narrative, she and the whole world became terrible to Penrod. He was sick.

His instinct was for flight; but flight through a town where he might anywhere encounter a policeman was impossible to consider. Therefore, he concealed himself. The sawdust box was his final refuge, and in it—having disposed of the incriminating badge—he burrowed beneath the surface of the saw-dust, and heaped it over him as bathers by the sea pile sand upon themselves.

Having become, in the shock of Marjorie's reve-lation, only Penrod Schofield, with not one whit of George B. Jashber or No. 103 remaining, he had found his situation more desperate than any he had ever been in before. Lovely Marjorie, herself, had be-come dreadful to him; his inwards shuddered as he thought of her prattling out his imaginings to her father. For the stricken Penrod now saw those imag-inings of his in a terrible light; they appeared as in-explicable lies that had brought about deadly results. He was unable to account for his conduct but could only review it fragmentarily and in agonized bewil-derment. Only once did any palliating excuse come to his mind, and that but feebly. "Anyway papa and mamma both said he was a horse-thief, and I heard 'em say it." But Marjorie's father had said that this must have been spoken in jest, and Penrod now recognized the probable correctness of such an ex-planation. In fact, he had long since realized within himself the fallibility of the theory that Mr. Dade made any part of his living by stealing horses. After this, no alleviating thought whatever was able to enter his mind.

What would they do to him? He had visions of a frightful Dade, tall as a tree, coming in vengeance, accompanied by Mr. Paoli Jones, Mr. Montgomery Jones and august policemen. He pictured such a group looking over the side of the sawdust box and bellowing at sight of him. He burrowed deeper, squirming.

At a sound from the street, he started violently; and there was sufficient cause, for it was the sound of an automobile gong, recognizable instantly as that of an ambulance—or a police car. It sounded closer, and Penrod was unable to remain in suspense. Trembling all over, he climbed out of the sawdust box and gazed forth from the woodshed door, allowing only his hair, his forehead and his eyes to be visible from outside.

A violently red open car came into sight upon the street, gonging passionately, and he was but little relieved when it passed by and whizzed away into inaudibility without having drawn up at the curb to let Mr. Dade, Mr. Paoli Jones, Mr. Montgomery Jones and the Chief of Police descend to search for him.

He returned to the box and burrowed again. Time
elapsed. It was a great hollow time of silence, hot
as the Sunday after Judgment Day. Penrod was wet
with perspiration, and sawdust was thick inside his
collar and down his back, upon his eyelids and in his
shoes, and he itched poignantly; but his other
troubles were immeasurably greater.

From afar, muffled by the sawdust, came the call
of Della, the cook: "Penrod! Musther Penrod! Penrod! Come in the house! Yer mother wants you to git
washed fer dinner. Musther Pen-*rod!*"

Silence.

"You better come, Musther Pen-*rod!*" The
kitchen door slammed; Della gave over.

Then, for another awful, hollow time, there was
silence.

XX

PROTECTIVE COLORATION

MEANTIME, Samuel Williams sped the gilded hours of the long summer afternoon by occupying himself in meritorious industry. He began this unusual procedure immediately after his self-defensive abandonment of Penrod; he requested a slight loan from his brother, Robert, in order to make a purchase of "dog-soap" at the grocery. Robert proved to be amiable in the matter, produced the sum of money required but offered an oblique comment.

"I didn't suppose anybody ever washed that sort of a dog, Sam."

"What? Why, John Carmichael deserves washing just as much as any dog does, and he needs it terribly. You can't hardly lead him anywhere, because he spends all his time trying to sit down and scratch behind his ear. He's got so that's almost the only thing he thinks about, and you can't get him to pay attention to anything else. I'm goin' to give him the finest bath any dog ever got in his life!"

This promise appeared to be perhaps a little over-liberal; but later it seemed to Robert that Sam was being as good as his word. The bath lasted two hours, as Robert was able to observe from the library bay-window, which commanded a view of the back yard, and Robert, seated near this window, found his attention frequently wandering from his book to the elaborate ablutions of John Carmichael. Sam bathed John Carmichael first by turning upon him a lively stream from the garden-hose; then he soaped John Carmichael heavily with the "dog-soap" and turned the stream from the garden-hose upon him again, until the soap surely must have disappeared, no matter how strongly it clung. After that, John Carmichael was placed in a wash-tub full of hot water brought from the kitchen in buckets; here, he was lathered again and rinsed pure again. Then the garden-hose was used upon him yet another time; he was soaped, then sprayed, then replaced in the tub, re-soaped, re-rinsed and once more sprayed. Robert began to fear that John Carmichael would be entirely washed away, for the astonished and obviously plaintive pup, in his wetness, looked unnaturally slight; but the drying was as thorough as the bathing. Sam brought forth from the house several torn bathtowels, and, with a protracted vigor of rubbing, restored John to his usual size and a better than normal appearance. The pup's spirits revived brilliantly, and, released, he placed his nose upon the ground between his forepaws, showed the whites of his eyes in wanton mockery, growled jocosely, then, leaping up suddenly, tore round and round the yard in apparently ferocious pursuit of a hundred phantoms.

Robert laughed, observing these high caperings; then, as his eye fell upon what his young brother was doing, his mouth opened and he sat in amazement. Sam, with a conscientious expression, carefully rinsed out the wash-tub, lugged it back into the cellar whence he had brought it, and reappeared with a large mop. With this implement, he soothed away the water from the spot upon the brick walk where the bathing had taken place; but he did not stop there. Evidently he thought that all of this walk needed cleansing, for he followed it, mopping the bricks slowly and carefully until he came near the bay-window, when Robert, addressing him through a fly-screen, interrupted his labors.

"What's the matter, Sam?"

"Matter? Nothin'. Why?"

"All this industry," the older brother explained. "Mopping up the walk when nobody's told you to."

"Well, there's a good deal of dust blows in from the street on this walk, and I'm goin' to give it a good moppin' clear around to the front gate."

"Voluntarily, Sam?" Then Robert had an after-thought as a relief to his sheer incredulity. "I see. Probably somebody did tell you to do it."

"They did not!" Sam returned, with indignation, and, in the same tone, he marvellously added, "I guess I like to feel I'm doin' some good in this world, don't I?"

"What!"

"I guess I'd like to be a little use once in a while before I die, wouldn't I?" Sam said, and he renewed his mopping with such honest vigor that he would have passed out of easy conversational distance if the astounded Robert had not again detained him.

"Sam, I've never seen anything like this before. Wait a minute! What have you been doing?"

Sam paused in his work to stare plaintively. "I been givin' my dog a bath and moppin' up our walk. Haven't you got any eyes?"

"Yes; that's what's puzzling me. You aren't looking for any special trouble when father comes home this evening—or anything like that, are you, Sam?"

"No, I am not!"

Robert's perplexity continued to be profound; but he tried a guess at random. "Nothing's gone wrong with that little matter we were talking about a couple of weeks ago, has it, Sam?" he asked, lowering his voice confidentially.

"What little matter?"

"You know. About Penrod Schofield's being a detective, and——"

"Penrod?" Sam interrupted, as if in surprise; but, even as he spoke, he looked away evasively and seemed to be interested in the upper branches of a young maple tree that grew flourishingly not far from the bay-window. "Penrod? I don't know anything much about Penrod and all that stuff you're talkin' about. I got my own business to 'tend to, so I don't know anything much about all that ole stuff."

"What!" his brother exclaimed. "Why Sam, you told me, yourself, that Penrod was *really* a detective!"

Sam continued to be interested in the top of the maple tree. "I b'lieve there's some ole bird or sump-thing got a nest up in the top of this tree," he said.

"Sam! Didn't you tell me that Penrod has a badge, and that——"

Sam allowed his gaze to descend from the sup-posititious bird's nest, and seemed to become inter-ested in polishing the handle of the mop with a corner of his jacket. "I guess maybe he did have some ole badge or sumpthing; but I don't expeck it amounts to much. Maybe he kind of thought he was a detec-tive—but just pretending, of course."

"But you said——"

"Me? Well, anyhow, if I kind of maybe did think so a little, it was just pretending, mostly, because he isn't one, and I guess he knows that much, himself. Anyhow, I guess he ought to by this time!" Sam spoke with cold severity, thus to detach himself still further from complications involving his friend. Moreover, he could not have explained, even to him-self, how it happened that he had previously be-lieved (at least to some extent) in the genuineness of Penrod's status as a detective, and now completely disbelieved that his comrade and leader had ever possessed any such official qualification. For Sam as well as for Penrod, Marjorie Jones's innocent communications had been shattering; from the moment when she had told them that her father spoke admiringly of Mr. Dade, and that her own unspeakable indiscretion in placing upon the adult plane George B. Jashber's revelations to her were causing Mr. Jones to begin actual grown-up investigations, the fiction that had seemed almost a reality to both boys instantly and hopelessly lost every vestige of substance. "I guess he hasn't got much sense," Sam added, speaking thus critically of his late chieftain. "But anyhow he ought to have enough to know that much."

To Robert, his small brother's tone seemed highly significant. "Is Penrod in trouble, Sam, about something or other?"

"Penrod? Not that *I* know anything about."

"Ah—about that matter, Sam——"Robert hesitated, and his tone became more confidential. "Have you four boys been keeping up the 'shadowing' you told me about?"

"Me?" Sam said reproachfully. "Why, you know, yourself, mamma wouldn't let me go out on account of the rain yesterday evening. I was right here in the house, and you know it as well as I do."

"Yes; but how about up to last night, Sam? How about when Mr. Dade has been at Mr. Schofield's in the evenings before last night? Haven't you all——"

"He hasn't been there," Sam said, with less caution. "He's only been there once since that Sunday afternoon you saw us and gave me fifty cents, and the next day you gave me a dollar more, but I had to give half of it to Penrod, and two dimes for Herman and Verman. That's about all you ever did give me, too," Sam added unnecessarily, "except on my birthday, maybe, or Christmas or sumpthing."

Robert disregarded this change of subject. "How do you know?" he asked. "How do you know Mr. Dade only came once after that?"

"Because it was the very next night," Sam informed him. "He and Margaret went in the house; but they left the window open, and she was talkin' kind of cross; but anyway he didn't stay long, and that's the last time he's been there yet, because— because——"

"Because what?" Robert inquired, as Sam hesitated.

But Sam felt that he might betray too much knowledge of Mr. Dade's movements. Robert had proved himself to be sympathetic; nevertheless, Robert was an adult and therefore might at any time suddenly hold inexplicable and punitive views; so reticence became advisable. "I don't know," Sam said, frowning. "I got this walk to clean up, Bob; I can't stand around here talkin' all afternoon."

"Yes; but listen——"

"I got to get this walk cleaned up the right way," Sam said, and applied the mop with earnest industry. "I got too much to do to stand around jibber-jabberin' with everybody day in and day out!"

Rebuffed and full of wonderment, Robert watched his brother's amazing performance of the unbidden task. Sam mopped the walk thoroughly all the way round to the front gate; then, with incredible thoughtfulness, he restored the mop to the cellar, and, emerging, brought the garden-hose to the front yard and began a systematic sprinkling of the lawn. He was thus engaged when his father returned home for the evening, and, after receiving words of surprised commendation from both of his parents, he quietly mentioned the fact that he had given the full length of the brick walk a careful mopping, and added, to their increased mystification, that he liked to feel he was doing some good in this world.

At the dinner-table his expression was dignified and modest, though perhaps a little self-consciously upright; possibly he might have blushed had he been aware how continuously he was the object of his older brother's inquiring, if furtive, scrutiny. Mr. Robert Williams's puzzlement (to which was naturally added some elation) increased with the passing hour, and so did his conviction that mysterious calamity threatened the band of sleuths of which his brother had been a member and Margaret's brother the chief. And when, after dinner, Sam went quietly into the library and sat down meekly with a book he had frequently been urged to read, Robert perceived that the pointed questions he wished to ask would be of little avail; yet he could not forbear some comment.

"I thought you had a prejudice against 'Pilgrim's Progress', Sam."

Sam looked up reproachfully, though it was observable that with the tail of his eye he noted the effect upon his father and mother, who sat near by, looking at him seriously over sections of the evening newspaper. "Did you?" he said gently. "Well, anyhow, I'm reading it. I like to feel——"

"Yes, I know," Robert interrupted. "Of course you like to feel you're doing some good in this world, Sam."

Sam did not like his brother's tone, which seemed to suppress with difficulty emotions of hilarity; but, before an exemplary retort could be devised, the telephone bell rang. The instrument was in another room and Robert went to answer it. Margaret Schofield's voice responded to his "Hello!"

"It's Mr. Williams, isn't it?" Margaret inquired, and Robert replied truthfully yet deceitfully, for he deepened and muffled his voice as he spoke:

"Yes—Mr. Williams."

"Mr. Williams, this is Margaret Schofield. Is Penrod there?"

"No. He hasn't been here."

"He hasn't? Not at all?"

"No, not at all."

"He wasn't there for dinner? We haven't been able to find him and we supposed that he was probably playing with Sam in the afternoon and stayed to dinner. I'm sorry to trouble you, but would you mind asking Sam if he knows where Penrod is?"

"Just a moment." Robert left the instrument and returned almost immediately to say, "Sam doesn't know. He says he hasn't seen Penrod since just after lunch. He says that Penrod went into the house to ask if he could go somewhere with little Marjorie Jones, and he doesn't know anything more about him."

"Thank you, Mr. Williams. Will you hold the wire just a moment longer, please!" Evidently Margaret engaged in a short conversation with other people near her; Robert heard several voices speaking simultaneously—a little urgently, too, though he could not distinguish what they said. Then she addressed him again: "Mr. Williams?"

"Yes; still here."

"If Sam isn't busy, do you suppose it would be too much trouble to ask him to come over here for a little while?"

"Not at all. I'll bring him, myself."

"Oh, no, you mustn't take all that trouble, Mr. Williams; but if Sam wouldn't mind coming——"

"Not at all. I'll bring him," Robert insisted, and, having clicked this interview to a close before Margaret could further protest, he returned to the library. "Hop up, Sam; they want you at Mr. Schofield's, and I'll go over there with you."

"Where?" Sam inquired sluggishly, not looking up from "Pilgrim's Progress".

"At Mr. Schofield's, I said. Come along!"

"What for?"

"I don't know. Probably because they can't find Penrod and think maybe you could help. Hop!"

Sam showed a strong disinclination to hop; he sank himself a little deeper in the luxurious armchair he occupied and increased his devout concentration upon "Pilgrim's Progress", his lips moving as he read.

"Sam!" Mrs. Williams said a little sharply. "You can read some more when you get back; we'll be delighted to let you sit up a little later than usual this evening, since you're so interested in a fine book; but if Mr. and Mrs. Schofield want you to help find Penrod it isn't polite to keep them waiting. Go along with Robert immediately."

Upon this, Sam saw that there was no help for it; he must go. He mumbled objections as long as he could, made delays, moved with outrageous deliberation—he consumed actual minutes in restoring "Pilgrim's Progress" to its exactly proper place in the book-case—and finally went so far as to suggest that he ought to wash his face and hands before leaving; but, as he had previously made himself noticeably immaculate, this unprecedented idea aroused serious parental impatience.

"You go with Robert this instant!" his father said.

Sam went; but as he and Robert approached their destination, his reluctance became so extreme that the older brother thought it the part of wisdom to walk with his hand affectionately upon the younger's shoulder. Margaret, looking serious and with a color already slightly heightened by recent episodes within the house, came to the door to admit them, and the sight of Robert obviously increased her embarrassment.

"Oh," she said blankly. "I thought it was Mr. Williams who——"

"It is," Robert returned with gravity. "I am Mr. Williams."

With that, and no more words upon the matter, he and his diffident charge followed her into the living-room, where sat in conclave apparently serious, Mr. and Mrs. Schofield, Mr. Paoli Jones and Marjorie. Beautiful little Marjorie occupied a sofa all to herself; she sat solemnly in the exact middle of it, and her lovely large eyes remained unmoved by the one side-glance she received from Sam as he came into the room.

XXI

INQUISITION

THE seriousness of the conclave was not perceptibly relaxed upon the entrance of the newcomers, although they were greeted hospitably and the warmness of the weather was mentioned, as they seated themselves in proffered chairs.

"We thought Sam might be able to help us out in one or two little matters," Mr. Schofield then explained. "But first we'd like to hear something more from him about where he thinks Penrod is. Little Marjorie, here, says she's almost sure that Sam knows."

Again Marjorie remained unmoved by the inscrutable side-glance of Master Williams, which remained upon her for a moment. "I bet he does," the lovely and terrible little girl said, with the utmost coolness. "I bet he knows where Penrod is this very minute and everything about the whole biznuss, besides. You ast him if he doesn't."

"Sam," Mr. Schofield said, "perhaps you didn't take time to think when you sent the message over the telephone that you didn't know where Penrod is. Now that you've had more time, don't you believe you could tell us, if you tried to?"

Sam swallowed painfully and fixed his gaze upon the toe of his right shoe, which moved slowly in a pattern it seemed to be tracing upon the floor. "Sir?" he said inquiringly.

Mr. Schofield looked somewhat annoyed, but repeated his question, adding, "I have an idea that Marjorie's right about it and that if you tried hard you could tell us where he is."

Sam's expression had become vacuous. "You mean where Penrod is, Mr. Schofield?"

"Oh, dear me!" Mr. Schofield said. "Oh, dear me!"

Upon this, Marjorie volunteered a suggestion. "I bet he does know. I bet I know, myself. I bet he's out in that ole sawdust box he goes to."

But Mr. Schofield shook his head. "No. Della said he wasn't there. She climbed up and looked inside and said there wasn't anything there except sawdust. Yet we're positive that he must be somewhere in the neighborhood; we're not at all uneasy about him, because he's sometimes absented himself like this before, when he's been in—ah—in difficulties, so to speak. He'll turn up after a while, of course; but the point is, we'd like to see him right now. You're sure you don't know anything about him, Sam?"

Here Robert felt that a slight intervention in Sam's behalf might serve to advance matters. "I doubt if Sam's in a position to know much about Penrod's present whereabouts, Mr. Schofield. Sam's been unusually busy at home all afternoon, as I can testify, myself. Perhaps, though," Robert added cheerfully, "there's something else you'd like him to enlighten you about?"

It was Mr. Jones, however, who took up this suggestion. "Yes," he said. "There is, indeed! As Marjorie has mentioned, Sam probably knows all about it, and in Penrod's absence it might be well for us to obtain the information from him. But as I imagine you're quite in the dark, yourself, Robert, as to what we're talking about, perhaps I'd better explain a little first, so that you'll understand. It concerns a gentleman who came to town before you returned home from college, I think. Perhaps you happened to meet him—a Mr. Herbert Hamilton Dade?"

"Dade?" Robert said inquiringly, and seemed to consider. "Dade. Ah—I think that I may have met him. At least I remember seeing him."

"Then you probably noticed that he was a very nice-looking young man," Mr. Jones said. "In fact, I'd call him quite a fine-looking young man. He came here with the idea that he would possibly settle down and go into business in our city, Robert, and he brought letters of introduction to me and to my brother, Montgomery. Perhaps you don't remember dear old Dr. Behring—he was the pastor of our church for many years but left here to accept a call from a church in Gosport, Illinois, about a decade ago—well, among the letters Mr. Dade brought was one from Dr. Behring. It was a most laudatory letter; Mr. Dade had been the Superintendent of Dr. Behring's Sunday-school for two years before leaving Gosport, and Dr. Behring testified in warm words to the young man's exemplary character. I must say that in every way Mr. Dade seemed to me to live up to the reputation Dr. Behring gave him. It's seldom, indeed, that one sees a young man of such good looks who so thoroughly appears to merit the extreme praise of a man like Dr. Behring, don't you think so, Mrs. Schofield?"

"Yes, indeed," she replied, with a glance at her husband, who looked a little embarrassed. "Go on, Mr. Jones, please, so that Robert will understand."

Mr. Jones obeyed. "I just wanted to be a little emphatic about the testimonial letter and the manner in which Mr. Dade seemed to me to live up to it. He took up his residence at the Y. M. C. A.; he joined our Sunday-school as a teacher, and everywhere, so far as I can learn, made the most excellent impression. As to his business, he had plans for forming a new insurance company and wished to interest my brother, Montgomery, and me in the project. In fact, we were interested and had begun to take the matter up with Mr. Dade quite seriously. Lately, however, both my brother and I noticed that the young man seemed to have grown curiously jumpy and nervous; it was obvious to us that he was becoming upset over something, and he appeared to be losing interest in the insurance business. Once or twice he spoke of possibly moving on to some other city with his project, and only a few days ago he surprised me in the middle of a quiet talk by jumping up and going to my office window in quite an excited way, and then breaking out at me, as if I'd annoyed him, and saying, 'My goodness! I can organize an insurance company in any other town just as well as I can here!' Of course I began to think then that he might decide to leave town; but I must say I didn't anticipate anything quite so abrupt as this." Mr. Jones paused to draw from an inner pocket a letter. "I'll read it to you, Robert, although the others have already heard it. It is simply Mr. Dade's farewell upon leaving town."

"Upon leaving town?" Robert repeated, and, with an effort almost visible, kept his gaze fixed upon Mr. Jones. "You—you mean Mr. Dade has left town— ah—permanently!"

"Permanently," Mr. Jones replied. "He writes as follows: 'I am returning to Gosport upon an early morning train and have concluded to remain there at home, where there will probably be little difficulty in forming the company in which I have endeavored to interest you and your brother, though of course the field is somewhat smaller. I take this step advisedly, having considered it for some time past. The climate of your city does not agree very well with my constitution, and although I have been most warmly welcomed here in many cordial circles, I believe the social advantages are nevertheless in favor of Gosport, and of course in selecting a permanent residence, such a consideration must be given due weight. Also, my health must naturally receive the first consideration, and in view of this city's unfavorable climatic situation I do not feel that I should defer my departure any longer. Thanking you for many courtesies and your appreciative consideration of the Reverend Doctor Behring's opinion of my character, I remain etcetera, etcetera'." Mr. Jones looked up from the reading. "A very remarkable letter," he observed gravely.

"Is it?" Robert asked, in a deferential tone. "I don't seem to see why—not exactly. He explains that the climate—and—the social conditions——"

"I mean it's remarkable under the circumstances, Robert," Mr. Jones explained. "That's what I've been coming to. At lunch to-day I was speaking regretfully to my wife of Mr. Dade's departure and happened to say what a nice young man he appeared to be, when we noticed that Marjorie was making unpleasant faces, and then, when we reproved her, she told us the most extraordinary story. She said Mr. Dade wasn't nice; he was a bad man—a terribly bad man. When we questioned her she said that Penrod had told her Mr. Dade stole horses. Of course we laughed; but she insisted that Penrod had heard both his mother and father declaring that Mr. Dade stole horses. Well, we've just been talking about that, and Mr. Schofield can't recall any such conversation; but Mrs. Schofield dimly remembers that she and Mr. Schofield made some jocular allusions once upon a time to horse-thieves having good manners in connection with the notably polished manners of Mr. Herbert Hamilton Dade, and she thinks Penrod may possibly have overheard them and taken the allusions literally. But this isn't the gist of the matter; it doesn't explain the rest of it. Penrod told Marjorie he had absolute information that Mr. Dade swindled people by getting them to sign papers; he told her Mr. Dade intended to get my brother, Montgomery, and me to 'sign papers' which would ruin us. Now, for one thing, in view of the fact that my brother and I would actually have signed quite a number of papers, if we'd concluded to join Mr. Dade in his insurance project, we couldn't help wondering if Penrod had somewhere heard some absurd rumor that ought to be stopped before it went any further."

"I should think that unlikely," Robert said judicially. "At least I haven't, myself, happened to hear of any grown-up rumor or libel attaching to Mr. Dade's undeniably excellent character. I should think it unlikely, sir."

"Yes, possibly," Mr. Jones returned. "But there's something else that has considerably mystified us, and it would be a satisfaction to get at the roots of the whole affair. Here's a sample of what's been happening: one day last week, Montgomery and Mr. Dade were walking along the street together, and Mr. Dade gave a perceptible start and uttered exclamations under his breath. It was broad daylight; the streets were full of people, and my brother naturally asked what was the matter. Mr. Dade was plainly excited and took my brother by the arm. 'Do you see that small, tongue-tied negro boy?' he asked. My brother looked around. 'I see a little negro boy; but I don't know whether he's tongue-tied or not,' he said. 'Well, he is,' Mr. Dade told him, almost angrily. 'He is tongue-tied!' That's all he would say about it; he insisted upon changing the subject, and Montgomery thought the incident very odd, indeed."

"It seems so," Robert said. "Go on, Mr. Jones."

"I will. You see, we seem to have a clue to a possible explanation, and that's what we want to get at. Marjorie says Penrod told her he was 'after' the wicked Mr. Dade and was 'shadowing' him. She tells us that he often plays with two small colored boys and that one of them is tongue-tied, so you see the suggestion, don't you, that appears to indicate a possible explanation of that bit of nervousness on the part of the young man—perhaps an explanation of more of his nervousness, besides? You see, Robert?"

"Well—in a way," Robert replied slowly. "Yes—in a way."

"It's all quite a mysterious business," Mr. Jones said. "It seems to me we ought to account for it if we can, and, since Penrod is temporarily missing, I thought that Sam, being his most intimate friend and usually mixed up in everything with him, might shed some light."

"I should think that might be entirely possible," Robert agreed. "What about it, Sam?"

Sam was still engaged in making patterns upon the floor with the toe of his shoe. "Me?" he said vaguely. "What about?"

"'What about'?" Robert returned, with some sharpness. "Why about what Mr. Jones has been talking about!"

"Oh!" Sam said, with the air of a polite person somewhat bored by information in which he has no personal concern. The little company waited; but he said nothing further.

"Now, Sam——" Robert began; but Mrs. Schofield intervened.

"Let me try," she said pleasantly. "Sam, I'm sure you won't mind answering some questions from me, will you?"

"No, ma'am."

"Well, then, you heard everything that Mr. Jones has been telling us, and we want you to say just what you know about it. You'll surely do that for *me*, won't you, Sam?"

"Yes, ma'am."

"Well, then, what *do* you know about it, Sam?"

"Ma'am?"

"Here, let me!" Mr. Schofield interposed impatiently. "Sam, you heard what Mr. Jones said about a little tongue-tied colored boy, didn't you?"

"Yes, sir."

"Very good! Now we intend to get at this whole business; but first we want you to tell us what you know about that little tongue-tied colored boy's making Mr. Dade nervous by following him. Speak up!"

Sam decided that it would be better for him not to say "Sir?" A slight frown appeared upon his brow, as though he engaged himself in thought; then he inquired: "Which little tongue-tied colored boy do you mean, sir?"

"Good heavens! I mean the one that——" Mr. Schofield began, but paused to pass a handkerchief over his exasperated brow; then he turned to Robert. "Here! He's your brother. Can't you get anything out of him?"

"I think so," Robert said, and, in a sharply business-like tone, took up the investigation. "See here, Sam! This shilly-shallying is only making matters worse and can't do you a particle of good. Everybody here understands that the little tongue-tied colored boy didn't do whatever he did to poor Mr. Dade of his own volition. That is to say, he didn't invent it, himself. Little Marjorie says that you and Penrod and those two colored boys from the alley— and we all know that one of them is tongue-tied—she says you were all engaged in an inexcusable performance that became very bothersome to this poor Mr.

Dade. Now we all know that, Sam, and, as I said, it isn't doing you any good to evade our questions. You know perfectly well that you and Penrod and the two colored boys from the alley were pretending that you were detectives and 'shadowing' poor Mr. Dade. There isn't a bit of good in your not admitting it."

"I didn't do anything," Sam returned plaintively. "I didn't have a thing to do with getting it up. I was away at Uncle Henry's farm when a good deal of it happened. I couldn't help what happened while I wasn't even in this ole town, could I?"

"Ah! Now we're getting somewhere!" Robert said, stating a fact that he was shortly to regret; then he increased the severity of his tone. "You admit, Sam, that you four boys were pretending that poor Mr. Dade was a criminal, and that you were——"

But here Robert proved incautious; for the moment, he had forgotten something important, of which he was now reminded, to his far from imperceptible confusion. "*You* said it was every bit all right," the badgered Sam interrupted suddenly. "You gave us a dollar and seventy cents for doing it!"

"What!" Three people, Mr. and Mrs. Schofield and Mr. Jones, uttered the word almost simultaneously, and Margaret leaned forward to ask, "What? What did you say, Sam?"

"He did!" Sam declared vehemently, roused to active defense by his resentment of Robert's outrageous double-dealing. "He gave me two quarters, first, to tell him about it, and after that, he gave me half-a-dollar and half-a-dollar for Penrod and two dimes for——"

"Never mind, Sam," Robert interrupted hastily; but the suffusion of color upon his cheeks made his face almost painfully conspicuous, as he spoke. With some difficulty he produced a poor imitation of the conventional murmur of laughter usually employed to indicate that the matter being mentioned is of negligible importance. "Perhaps I should explain that at the time Sam is speaking of what the boys were doing appeared to be merely a little game among themselves and—ah—perfectly harmless, of course."

"Indeed?" Miss Margaret Schofield inquired, with evident interest. "Perfectly harmless?"

"Ah——" he began; but he neither met her inquiring gaze nor found anything more to say, and an embarrassing silence fell upon the room.

Mr. Paoli Jones, however, being a humane person,

relieved the tension by coughing, and then by a return to the previous subject. "Perhaps we might get on a little better if we followed another lead," he suggested. "I mean if we could determine conclusively the identity of the little tongue-tied colored boy——"

But once more it was proven that coincidences abound at critical moments in the lives of all who conduct criminal investigations, and a peculiarly striking one took place at this instant and while Mr. Paoli Jones still had the phrase "little tongue-tied colored boy" upon his lips. The windows were open, and upon the aromatic zephyrs of the July evening was borne an eerie and giggling cry in a unique African voice.

Mrs. Schofield started. "Listen!" she whispered huskily.

From a distance of about forty feet, the strange cry came distinctly. "Oh Mihhuh Habe im air? Wop he boo mow, Pemwob?"

It was unfortunate for Penrod that Verman felt this renewal of interest in the whereabouts and conduct of the official ex-criminal of the dismembered agency. Penrod had emerged to the surface, necessarily, as soon as Della stopped looking over the top of the sawdust box; under cover of darkness he had abandoned that refuge, and, for the past hour, seated upon the ground beneath one of the living-room windows, he had listened anxiously to the conversation within. Verman, with idle time upon his hands, for the first time in many evenings, had gone forth for a stroll, and, glancing over the fence, had happened to espy the dark figure under the window. Then, having nothing better to do, he climbed upon the fence and sat there. Amused, and not being aware that the agency was now wholly obsolete, he had been so ill-inspired as to put the inquiry that had startled the company indoors, his intended words being simply: "Old Mr. Dade in there? What he do now, Penrod?"

Penrod made imperative gestures for him to withdraw, then sprang up and, alarmed by something he heard from within the living-room, would himself have withdrawn; but he was too late. Mr. Schofield, easily recognizing the significance of the vocative, "Pemwob", had dashed out through the front door, turned the corner of the house, and the fugitive was almost instantly seized in a powerful and irritated grasp. One minute later, when, in custody, he was haled into the presence of the conclave, his mother uttered a shrill cry of lamentation. In spite of all his

woody immersions, fragments of the attic cobwebs
still remained upon him, and he shed a trail of sawdust across the living-room floor, as he was sternly
urged forward. What he expected to happen to him,
at this juncture, is unknown; his expression was
impenetrable; but there is no doubt whatever that
the substitution of him as the center of interest
brought grateful relief to both of the brothers
Williams.

"Never mind his looks!" Mr. Schofield said sharply
to Mrs. Schofield. "That can be attended to later—
and so can a few other things!" he added. "Later
when I take him upstairs——"

But Mr. Paoli Jones, as he had already proved,
was a man of humane impulses, and he could not look
at Penrod without having those impulses stirred.
"No, no," he said, protesting. "I really didn't mean
to get either Sam Williams or Penrod into any
trouble; I only wanted to satisfy my own mind a
little about what's been happening, and I think that
has become rather clear. In fact, it seems to me that
what Robert said about it's all having been merely a
harmless game was especially significant." Here Mr.
Jones laughed and looked genially, not at Robert, but
at Margaret Schofield, upon which she straightened

and seemed a little indignant. "It appears to be fairly evident," Mr. Jones went on, "that Penrod and Sam and the two colored boys were merely playing at 'shadowing', and that they felt they had to pick out someone to be 'shadowed', and of course this person had to be supposed to be in the habit of committing crimes. I think I see now that this explanation covers everything Penrod told Marjorie, and that he was only carrying on the game and never dreamed she would repeat what he said as serious information. In fact, I don't believe there's anything serious at all in the whole matter; quite probably Mr. Dade might have gone back to Gosport anyhow; in his letter he speaks of the 'social advantages' Gosport possesses, compared to this city, and in that respect he may have suffered some little disappointment or other here. That's quite possible—quite possible, in spite of the fact of his good looks and excellent conduct. But there is one thing that puzzles me and that I'd like to have solved. In fact, there's a question I'd very much like to have Penrod answer."

"He'll answer it," Mr. Schofield promised grimly. "I'll see to that!"

"Well, then," Mr. Jones said, addressing Penrod, "I'd like to know why it was that when you picked out a person to be 'after', as you told Marjorie, Penrod—that is, when you selected a criminal to 'shadow', how in the world did it happen that you selected a young man of such unexceptional and exemplary character as Mr. Dade?"

"Sir?"

"Why on earth did you select such a good young man as Mr. Dade to be your criminal?"

Penrod swallowed, and moved uneasily, causing a little shower of sawdust to fall upon the floor about him. "Well——" he mumbled, and stopped.

"You speak up!" his father said, in a tone recognizably ominous. "You answer Mr. Jones's question! What made you pick out Mr. Dade?"

"Yes, Penrod," Mr. Jones urged, rising to go. "Why did you?"

Penrod breathed deeply; he had not an idea in his head. "Well——" he said at last, desperately. "Well —he acted so in love of my sister Margaret, I thought there must be sumpthing wrong with him."

Mr. Jones stared at him strangely, seeming unwilling to trust himself to speak; there was a sound like the sputter of laughter, half-choked and a little hysterical, from the corner to which Robert Williams had modestly retired; then Margaret, after the

briefest and coldest glance in that direction, rose
and went haughtily out to the verandah.

"I think we must say good-night," Mr. Jones said
in a tremulous voice, during this progress. "Come,
Marjorie." His face had grown red, and, in passing
Mr. Schofield, who likewise had become flushed, he
paused to say in a low tone, with a glance toward
Penrod, "I hope you won't——"

But it was Mrs. Schofield who replied to this merci-
ful plea. She, too, displayed a heightened color, and
she spoke indistinctly through a handkerchief held to
her mouth. "No," she said, shaking her head, "he
won't."

Then, as the departing guests moved on toward
the outer door, Mr. and Mrs. Schofield hospitably
accompanying them, the little group was passed by
Robert Williams on his way to the verandah, and
Penrod and Sam were left alone together in the
living-room. Somehow, they realized an impending
darkness had lightened; a vague doom inexplicably
incurred had as inexplicably been avoided. Neither
understood what sin he had committed or not committed; neither understood why punishment was com-
muted. Definitely they had only the sense of a vast
escape.

Sam, again making patterns upon the floor, seemed to be preoccupied with the moving toe of his shoe, while Penrod shook down a little more sawdust and stood gazing at it gloomily. They said nothing whatever.

XXII

NEW STARS ARISE

THE midsummer morning was languid with its own warmth; the Schofields' back yard lay aglow in mellow sunshine, and Penrod and Sam stood enthralled, staring at a magnificent creature they had discovered upon the stalk of a lush bush in the fence corner. It might have been a pixie's concertina, painted dusty green and ornamented with brilliant pool balls from a pixie pool table; but to Penrod and Sam it was known as a "tobacco-worm"—the largest and fattest they had ever seen.

The two boys stared in silence for a long time; finally, Penrod spoke in a hushed voice.

"I wonder what he's thinkin' about." And in fact, it was reasonable to suppose the motionless creature lost in reverie.

"Thinkin' about how fat he is, maybe," Sam suggested.

"I bet you don't know which end his head is," said Penrod, his tone somewhat implying that this wagered bit of ignorance was one of Sam's many inferiorities.

"I bet you don't, either."

"Well, whoever said I did?" Penrod retorted crossly.

"Well, did *I* say *I* did?"

"Well, whoever said you did say you did?"

Sam looked annoyed and also somewhat confused. "Well, you said," he began, "you said I didn't know which end his head is, and I——"

"Well, you *don't* know which end his head is."

"Well, you don't, either."

"Well, whoever said I did?"

"Well, *I* didn't say *I*——"

"Well, whoever said you did say you did?"

"Look here——" Sam began; but paused, bewildered

by that feeling of having done the same thing before, which inclines people, sometimes, to believe in the theory of reincarnation.

A movement on the part of the green creature distracted the attention of both boys, momentarily, from their incipient feud.

"Look!" Penrod cried. "He's movin'!"

"Climbin' up the bush," Sam observed. "That shows which end his head is on: it's on top."

"It doesn't have to be on top just because he's climbin' up the bush," Penrod returned scornfully. "I guess he could back up, just as well as climb up, couldn't he?"

"Well, he wouldn't," Sam argued. "What would he want to back up for, when he could just as easy climb up? His head's on top of him, and that proves it."

"It doesn't either prove it. Where's his face? The only way you can prove where his head is, is where his face is, isn't it?"

"No, it isn't!" Sam cried hotly. "He hasn't got any face; and, besides, his top end looks just as much like his face as his bottom end. You can't tell the difference. Anyway, anybody with good sense would know his head's on top of him. He wouldn't *want* to have it any place else, would he?"

"How do *you* know what he'd want?" Penrod demanded. "He might want it some place else just as well as not."

"Well, what for?" Sam asked irritably. "What on earth would he want it some place else *for*?"

"What for?" Penrod was sure of a coming triumph in the debate. "You don't know what for?"

"No, I don't, and you don't either!"

"Oh, I don't, don't I?"

"No, you *don't!*" Sam shouted.

Penrod laughed pityingly. "Bet you I can prove it."

"Well, prove it then."

"Well, look here. Suppose sumpthing was *after* him: he'd want to have his face on his bottom end so's he could keep watchin' out to see if it was comin' after him up the stalk, wouldn't he? *That* proves it, I guess!"

It did—so far as Sam Williams was concerned. Sam was overwhelmed; he had nothing to say, and Penrod was not disposed to make his triumph an easy one for the vanquished. "Well," he jeered. "I guess that shows how much you know about *worms!*"

Sam had the grace to admit a fair defeat. "Maybe

I don't," he said, with manly humbleness; "—about tobacco-worms. I don't suppose I ever saw more'n five or six in my life." He dug the ground with the toe of his shoe, despondently, then brightened, all at once, with the advent of a recollection. "I bet I know sumpthing about grasshoppers that you don't."

"I bet you don't."

"Well, I can prove it."

"Go ahead and prove it!"

"I bet you don't know grasshoppers chew tobacco."

At this, Penrod yelled in derision.

"They do, too!" Sam asserted indignantly.

Penrod laughed, gesticulated, danced and bellowed. He was outrageous.

"You wait!" Sam began to browse in the grass, searching, while his friend, in order to express a poignant incredulity, threw himself full-length beneath the bush; rolled on his stomach, squealed insults, beat the ground with his hands and wriggled his feet in the air.

"Grasshoppers chew tobacco!" howled Penrod. "Grasshoppers chew tobacco! Grasshop—oh, ho, ho, ho!"

"Here," said Sam, bringing a grasshopper for his

inspection. "You watch him, now." He gave the grasshopper a command, squeezed him slightly about the middle, and proved the case absolutely. "Look there!" he cried, flourishing the exhibit upon his thumbnail. "*Now*, say grasshoppers don't chew tobacco!"

Penrod was beside himself but not (as would have been proper) with confusion: ecstasy was his emotion —and there followed a bad quarter-of-an-hour for the grasshoppers in that portion of the yard.

"Pshaw!" said Sam. "I've known grasshoppers chewed tobacco ever since I was five years old."

"You never *said* anything about it!" Penrod exclaimed, marveling at such reticence. It seemed to him, just now, that he would never know another instant of ennui so long as he lived—at least, not in grasshopper-time.

"I thought pretty near everybody knew grasshoppers chewed tobacco," Sam said modestly. "You told me I didn't know much about worms, and I said I bet I knew sumpthing about grasshoppers you didn't know—but I kind of thought you did, though."

"What else can they do?" Penrod's tone indicated that a sincere deference was no more than Sam's due in all matters concerning grasshoppers.

"Nothin'. That's all they're good for."

"Where d'you s'pose they get their tobacco in the first place? Hop around stores, you guess?"

"Yes; lots of other places."

The experiment had been repeated *ad nauseam* until all the available grasshoppers were in no condition immediately to pursue their bad habits—or their good ones, for that matter—and Penrod paused to seek further knowledge at its recent fountain-head. "Sam, do you know anything else?" he inquired hopefully.

"Yes, I do!" replied Master Williams with justified resentment.

"I mean," Penrod explained, "I mean: Do you know anything else I don't know?"

"Oh!" Sam was mollified at once. "Well, I guess proba'ly I do," he said thoughtfully. "Lemme see. Oh, yes! I bet you don't know if you put a black hair from a horse's tail in a bottle and put water in it, and leave it there for three weeks, it'll turn into a snake."

"I do, too!" said Penrod. "I knew *that*, ever since I was little."

"I bet you haven't known it any longer'n I have. I knew it when I was little, too."

"Everybody knows a black hair from a horse's tail will turn into a snake," Penrod declared. "Who doesn't know *that?*"

"Well, I never said they didn't, did I?"

"Well, who said you did say——" Penrod paused, a sudden light in his eyes. "Sam, did you ever *try* it?"

"No," said Sam thoughtfully. "I guess when I heard it we didn't have any horse, and I was too little to get one from any other people's horse—or sumpthing."

Penrod jumped up eagerly. "Well, we aren't *too* little now!" he shouted.

"*Yay!*" This jubilant outcry from Sam demonstrated what reciprocal fires of enthusiasm were kindled in his bosom on the instant. "Where's a horse?"

Simultaneously their eyes fell upon what they sought. In the side street stood a grocer's wagon, and the grocer had just gone into the kitchen. Attached to the wagon was an elderly bay horse. Attached to the elderly bay horse was a black tail. The prospective snake manufacturers drew near the raw material.

The elderly bay horse switched his black tail at a fly, a gesture unfortunate for Penrod, upon whose eager countenance it culminated. "Oof!" He jumped back, sputtering; and the horse looked round inquiringly; then, seeing boys, assumed an expression of implacable fury.

"Go on," Sam urged. "Pull 'em out. Two's enough."

Penrod rubbed his face and looked thoughtful. "I wonder if they wouldn't do just as well from his mane," he said.

"No, sir! They got to be from his tail. I know *that* much!"

Penrod glanced uneasily at the horse's horizontal ears. "You pull 'em, Sam," he suggested, edging away. "I'll go and be gettin' the bottles ready to put 'em in. I——"

"No, sir!" Sam insisted. "You started to pull 'em and you ought to do it. I didn't start to pull 'em, did I?"

"Now, see here!" Penrod became argumentative. "You don't know where to find any bottles, and——"

"You better quit talkin' so much," Sam interrupted doggedly. "Go ahead and pull those two hairs out of his ole tail or pretty soon the man'll come out and drive him away—and then where'll we be? You started to do it, and so it's your biznuss to. Go ahead and do it, and don't talk so much about it. That's the way to do a thing."

"Well, I am goin' to, ain't I?"

"*Now!*" Sam exclaimed. "He's quit lookin' at us. Quick!"

Seizing this opportunity, Penrod ventured the deed and was rewarded. The elderly horse seemed to have forgotten his animosity; his mood had become one of depression merely; he hung his head, and marked the ravishment by nothing more than a slight shudder. "There!" said Penrod; and, as they went back into the yard, he glanced disdainfully at the gloomy quadruped. "It's easy to get hairs out of a horse's tail for a person that knows the right way to do it. I bet I could of pulled his whole tail out!"

But this was only a thought in passing, and the attention and energies of both boys were now devoted to the preliminaries of their great experiment. The largest empty bottles obtainable were selected, cleaned and filled with fair water. Then, with befitting solicitude, the two long black hairs were lowered into the water, and the bottles were corked. After that, a label was pasted upon each, exhibiting the owner's name and address. The fascinating work was not complete, however; Penrod paid a visit to the kitchen clock, and, after some severe exercises in computation, the following note was inscribed in precise duplicate upon the labels:

"Hair from Jacop R. Krish and Cos horse tail put in sixteen minutes of evelen oclock July 11 Snake comes sixteen minutes of evelen oclock July 32."

They set the bottles, side by side, upon an empty box in the former office of George B. Jashber; stood before them; gazed upon them.

"Don't you wish they'd turn right now?" Penrod said yearningly. "I don't see why it's got to be three weeks."

"Well, it has."

"I know that; but I wish it didn't *haf* to be. Well, anyway, three weeks from now we'll be lookin' at our good ole snakes, all right!"

"Three weeks from now!" Sam echoed, with luscious anticipation. "Yes, sir! *Oh*, oh!"

"What'll we feed 'em?"

"I don't know. Suppose they'll want to come out of the bottles?"

"You bet they will! I'm goin' to train mine to follow me all around the yard. When school begins maybe I'll take him with me in my pocket."

"*Oh*, oh!" cried Sam. "So'll I."

They shouted with joy of the picture.

"I wouldn't take a million dollars for mine!" said Penrod.

"Neither would I!" said Sam. "I wouldn't take two million!"

"Neither would I!"

Then, fascinated, Penrod sat down upon the stable floor close to the box upon which stood the precious bottles, and Sam likewise sat, each gazing earnestly upon his own bottle and its slender occupant. Thus they remained for some time, silently engaged in who can say what paternal speculations; minute bubbles had already appeared upon the submerged hairs, and, to a gaze long fixed, faint stirrings and movements seemed almost perceptible; or, at least, such first tokens of transformation were easily imaginable.

"Sam, I believe mine's begun to breathe already," Penrod whispered.

"Sh!" Sam warned him, and so concentrated was the attention of Master Williams that he did not move when a heavy breath disturbed the short hair on the nape of his slender neck just above the collar. A moment later, however, as the same spot was affectionately caressed by something that felt like a banana peeling that had been dipped in warm water, he decided that too great a liberty was being taken with him. "You go away from here!" he hissed fiercely.

Without resentment, Walter-John returned to the doorway of the stable, which he had just entered, accompanied by a congenial friend, and for some moments the two communed inaudibly through the nose. Then Walter-John yawned inoffensively, although the action was taken in Duke's very face, which was close enough to be almost involved within the cavern; after that, both dogs moved drowsily away from the rhomboid of hot sunshine near the doorway and sought the cooling shade of the interior. Duke stretched himself, then reclined upon his back, and Walter-John, approaching, let himself down awkwardly, and for his heavy head confidingly used the older and much smaller dog's stomach as a pillow. This, Duke found inconvenient, even annoyingly burdensome; he complained crossly, removed himself and lay elsewhere, while Walter-John looked at him reproachfully with one eye, then closed it and slept with his chin upon the floor.

At the sound of Duke's brief vocal complaint, Sam said "Sh!" again, after which the fascinated silence where the miracle worked within the stable obediently became complete; but there were noises outside that grew louder, and before long were too disturbing to be overlooked. In the alley Herman and Verman were playing vociferously with a rubber ball, and, not content with shouting almost continuously, they presently began to throw the ball against the doors of the carriage-house, evidently to catch it upon the rebound.

"My goodness!" Penrod said indignantly. "Haven't they got *any* sense?" And finding the thumping of the ball unendurable, he went to the carriage-house doors, threw them open and shouted angrily: "My goodness! Don't you know anything at *all!*"

Surprised, Herman and Verman came to the doorway. "Whut you mad fer?" Herman inquired mildly. "Whut all goin' on you git so mad, Penrod?"

"Never mind," Penrod said coldly. "We got sumpthing on our hands here we don't want any ole ball bangin' and whangin' up against these doors!"

"Whut all you got goin' on you ack so big, Penrod?"

"Never mind!"

But Verman had already entered the stable, and Herman followed, urged by a natural curiosity, which both Penrod and Sam plainly found annoying. "My goodness!" Sam exclaimed. "What do you haf to come hangin' around here now for, makin' all this noise? Why can't you take your ole ball up the alley and play where we don't haf to listen to you? Haven't you got sense enough to know how to tell when we're busy?"

To be the more impressive, he frowned heavily as he spoke, and the severity of his expression evidently interested Verman. "Wop he mek fafe fo?" the smaller brother inquired of the larger.

"Verman want to know why you makin' faces," Herman translated, chuckling. "You look so mad Verman think you tryin' to make him laugh."

Upon this, Sam frowned so heavily that Verman did laugh; delighted, he pointed at Sam's face and also at Penrod's, for Penrod was frowning as darkly. Verman squealed hilariously, and then, sobering somewhat, he gave utterance to a thought that deepened the annoyance of the two white boys by its seeming sheer irrelevancy. "Oo dum kef oh Mihhuh Habe yip?"

"He want to know ef you done ketch ole Dade yit," the faithful interpreter explained.

"Oh, my goodness!" Penrod said, and Sam said the same thing almost simultaneously. The two looked at each other, expressing in the glance their mutual hopelessness of so low an intelligence as that just displayed before them. Almost two weeks had elapsed since the hot day spent by Penrod in the sawdust box, principally, and by Sam in laudable, self-imposed tasks; for both of the friends mists of time had intervened, and all the affairs of the agency were dim with remoteness, almost lost over the horizon of the long, long ago. George B. Jashber was as extinct as last year's first day of school. "Oh, my goodness!" Penrod exclaimed again, turning upon Verman. "Don't you know anything at *all*? Why, Mr. Dade doesn't even live in this town any more!"

But Verman received this scornful information without any emotion; he was not interested, for he had observed the two bottles upon the box before which the annoyed Sam still continued to sit. "Wop ap?"

He stretched forth a small brown hand toward Sam's bottle; but, before the shining glass could be violated by this ignorant touch, Sam pushed him away, and said angrily, "You get back! For heaven-ses' sakes, can't you keep away from here? If you dare to stick your ole hand near this bottle, I'll——"

But Verman was already giggling again, and Herman, too, seemed to be highly amused, so that their united laughter drowned out the sound of Sam's voice. "Makem hake!" Verman squealed, jumping up and down and clapping the pinks of his hands together. "Makem hake! Makem hake!"

"Cert'nly, we're makin' snakes!" Penrod shouted fiercely. "And you quit makin' all that noise in here. You think we want our good ole snakes ruined by everybody comin' in here and yelling and everything? You think our snakes are goin' to begin turnin' with all this noise and——"

"Noise ain' go' hurt no snakes," Herman interrupted, abating his laughter but little. "Ain' go' be no snakes. You cain' make no snakes less'n you put hoss hairs in a bottle an' nev' look at 'em. You put hoss hair in a bottle an' nev' look once fer th'ee weeks you go' to git a snake. You ev' take one peep at hoss hair, snake done spoil'; ain' go' be no snake in nem bottles—nuff'm 'cep' hoss-tail hair."

"What!" Penrod shouted, and his attitude became so threatening that Herman retreated from him, protesting, though with continued laughter. "You get out o' here!" Penrod bellowed. "You get on out o' here! You don't know anything in this world, and you come round here tryin' to ruin these good ole snakes——"

"Lemme 'lone, whi' boy!" Herman begged, sputtering, as he moved toward the alley door. "I ain' done nuff'm to you. All I do, I dess say hoss-tail hair ain' go' turn into no snake ef you look at——"

"You get out o' here!" Penrod shouted, and he seemed to look about him for weapons or something to throw, whereupon, their merriment increasing, both Herman and Verman fled lightly with noiseless feet. Their voices, however, could still be heard as they sped down the alley, and the penetrating, silvery giggle of Verman came through the air for some little time longer to four ears reddened by irritation.

Penrod closed the alley doors, returned to the box and again sat down near Sam. "Never did have any sense," he muttered, alluding to the mirthful fugitives, and he added morosely, "Think they know so much!"

"Yes," Sam assented, in like mood. "Why, if I didn't know any more about snakes than Herman does, I'd sell out! I would; I'd sell out my whole biznuss and move away! He just said that to be smart, and because he and Verman haven't got any horse-tail hair, themselves—nor any good bottles to put 'em in, if they did have, proba'ly—and want to behave like they know everything on earth. Nobody that ever lived ever heard anything about not lookin' at 'em, so that proves it." His manner became argumentative. "Because, look here, Penrod—listen, Penrod—just lookin' at anything at all doesn't do anything to it. F'r instance, you could look all day at a tadpole and that wouldn't stop him from changin' into a frog, and you know that as well as I do; but you take Herman and he'd tell you if you had a tadpole and wanted him to change to a frog, you couldn't ever look at him or else he wouldn't."

"Yes, that's exackly what that ole Herman would say," Penrod agreed. "He wouldn't know any more about frogs than he would about snakes, because, listen, Sam: How could you put a horse-tail hair in the bottle, in the first place, without ever lookin' at it? I guess that proves he doesn't know anything he's talkin' about, doesn't it?"

"'Course it does!" Sam said, well pleased. "Colored people don't know anything, anyway."

To this prejudiced view of an amiable and interesting race, Penrod, in his present mood, offered no objection; instead, he frowned, pursed his lips and, so far as he was able, assumed an air of maturity and importance. "They don't know anything about anything," he said, in this manner. "I heard my father say, himself, that they're nothing but a mash of stuperstition."

"What?" Sam asked deferentially.

But Penrod felt it better to let well enough alone and not to attempt the phrase again. "I heard papa say it, myself," he said. "I guess that settles how much Herman knows about snakes, doesn't it?"

"It cert'nly does," Sam agreed, and then for a time they sat in silence, content in the faith that the matter was settled and Herman's unfounded and almost malicious criticism well answered. In the expression of each, as he gazed upon his own bottle's occupant, there was something like tenderness, a hint of the resentful fondness felt by one who has championed, defended and perhaps saved a helpless, loyal dependent. Minutes had elapsed when Sam uttered a muffled but excited exclamation. "Look, Penrod!" he whispered. "There's a new bubble come right at the top end of mine, where his face is goin' to be, because mine's goin' to have his face——"

"Sh!" Penrod interrupted sternly, but without

removing his gaze from his own bottle. "Can't you keep still? Sh!"

Duke and Walter-John, disturbed by the arrival of Herman and Verman, had moved out into the yard; but now, returning, they disposed themselves for slumber upon the stable floor at a little distance from their masters, and again Duke, forgetting to what burden he exposed himself, lay partially upon his back. Walter-John almost immediately seized the opportunity to employ the elderly dog's delicate stomach as a pillow, and Duke, too drowsy to move, uttered a few low and threatening complaints, for which he was angrily reproved in a husky whisper.

"You stop that!" Penrod thus commanded over his shoulder. "My goodness!"

Sam also looked round; upon which, Walter-John, without materially altering his posture, thought fit to wag his tail; but it was a tail already of some weight, and its wagging made a thumping upon the stable floor.

"You quit that!" Sam whispered ferociously. "My goodness!"

Walter-John, unreproachful and obedient, at once lay motionless, and Duke, though almost painfully incommoded by the other's naïve selfishness, was now too sleepy either to change his position or to make any further protest. A complete silence fell upon that place. Penrod and Sam, fascinated, sat gazing intently, each at his own hair from the tail of Jacob R. Krish and Company's horse.

From time to time, Duke, not otherwise moving, half opened one eye to let a glance of devotion rest momentarily upon Penrod. Similarly, Walter-John sometimes partly opened an eye to look affectionately at Sam.

THE END

BOOTH TARKINGTON

Ever since 1899 when Booth Tarkington, a young gentleman of leisure, first began to spend his days "fussin'
with literature," he has been concerned with the interpretation of American life. His books catch the spirit of
America as no other has caught it. His brilliant career
as a writer, each year bringing more remarkable success,
has seldom been equalled.

ALICE ADAMS

CLAIRE AMBLER

GENTLE JULIA

A GENTLEMAN FROM INDIANA

LITTLE ORVIE

THE MIDLANDER

MIRTHFUL HAVEN

MONSIEUR BEAUCAIRE

PENROD

PENROD AND SAM

PENROD JASHBER

PRESENTING LILY MARS

SEVENTEEN

THE TURMOIL

WANTON MALLY

GROSSET & DUNLAP

Publishers   New York

PETER B. KYNE'S NOVELS

Mr. Kyne is a globe-trotter and all the seven seas and the islands therein contribute color for the vivid stories of action and romance which come so readily to his pen. And these will be welcomed by the legion of readers who look to him for entertainment in an all around good story.

GROSSET & DUNLAP

Publishers   NEW YORK